NANCY WARREN

STITCHES
AND WITCHES

VAMPIRE KNITTING CLUB
BOOK TWO

ISBN: ebook 978-1-928145-50-9

ISBN: print 978-1-928145-49-3

Cover Design by Lou Harper of Cover Affair

Ambleside Publishing

INTRODUCTION

Dropping stitches and catching killers

When an older gentleman keels over in his scones and tea at the Elderflower Tea Shop in Oxford—a victim of poison—Lucy Swift and her band of undead amateur detectives are on the case.

Elderflower Tea Shop is next door to Cardinal Woolsey's, the yarn shop Lucy runs and home to the late-night Vampire Knitting Club. The tea shop owners are a pair of octogenarian spinsters and old family friends, so Lucy wants to help clear up the mystery that's keeping their shop closed. But murder isn't the only issue troubling the Miss Watts. A man has come between them. Miss Florence Watt is being romanced by an old flame, one Mary Watt distrusts.

In between figuring out who, among his many enemies, might have poisoned the unpleasant Colonel Montague, Lucy's trying to brush up on her magic spells before the Wiccan potluck dinner her witchy cousin insists she attend.

However, she's still settling into being a witch and since she botched a spell and blew up her kitchen, she's taking the magic slowly.

Her knitting endeavors aren't much better. Between purling when she should knit and dropping so many stitches her hand-knit scarf looks like it was attacked by giant moths, there are days Lucy thinks she'll pack it all in and move back to Boston. She might, except she'd miss her beloved undead grandmother, her new friends, one very sexy vampire and a local detective who is very much alive.

Stitches and Witches is Book 2 in the Vampire Knitting Club series of paranormal cozy mysteries. It is a standalone novel with no sex or gore, just humor, knitting, magic and a touch of romance.

STITCHES AND WITCHES

CHAPTER 1

The gentleman who walked into Cardinal Woolsey's Knitting Shop that October morning reminded me of a character actor. Not one you can immediately name, but one who plays generals and titled English gentlemen. He'd have had bit parts in *Downton Abbey* and Jane Austen adaptations with his white, wavy hair, perfectly trimmed mustache and twinkling blue eyes. He was tanned as though he'd spent the last few months in the south of France. He wore a tweed sports jacket, gray flannels and sported a silk cravat around his neck.

My first impression of him was that he was quite tall, but when I looked again I realized it was his upright bearing that made him seem taller than he was. The term larger-than-life went through my head. He didn't appear to be a knitter but, as I'd discovered through running Cardinal Woolsey's for the last few weeks, knitters came in all shapes and sizes, ages and sexes.

Some were even vampires.

"Good morning," I said, stepping out from behind the counter.

When he saw me, his face lit up as though we were old friends, even though I was certain I'd never seen him before. His teeth were quite large, white and straight. "Good morning," he replied. "And it's a good morning indeed when I'm greeted by a beautiful young woman."

He said the words in a casual way as though he paid extravagant compliments to every woman—young or old, pretty or plain. I was about to ask him if he was handy with the needles, when he said, "I've come to throw myself on your mercy."

I blinked at the choice of words and then from the twinkle in his eye realized he wasn't serious.

He took a deep breath. "It's about a woman who used to live next door at the Elderflower Tea Shop. Her name was Florence Watt."

I sensed intrigue. Florence and Mary Watt were spinster sisters who had been running Elderflower Tea Shop next door for a long time, probably since tea first came to England. I got the feeling this man had known Florence many years ago. Did he think perhaps she had married and changed her name?"

I put him out of his misery. "Miss Watt is still next door. She and her sister, Mary, run the tea shop."

He put a hand to his heart. "And is it possible that Miss Florence Watt is unattached?"

It was strange to think of either of the Miss Watts as having a romantic life, and yet, it seemed at one time there must've been one. I tried not to look nosy but I don't think I succeeded.

"You've guessed it, of course. I loved Florence fifty-five years ago and I've never been able to forget her."

I'd read of such cases. High school sweethearts who reunited in their golden years, couples who'd been kept apart by circumstance and got together late in life. I was excited to play even a small role in a golden age romance.

Even though it was difficult to imagine the practical and efficient Florence Watt as a young woman in love, I was a romantic at heart and wanted to think she might still find love.

I was curious, and he seemed eager to talk about his affairs. Since it was a quiet morning in the shop, I'd be quite happy to put off doing inventory for another few minutes. "You must have been very young."

He nodded, and gazed in the direction of the tea shop. "Hardly more than a boy. But there was something about Florence that I had never seen in another girl. We fell in love, and I believed I'd found the woman I would spend the rest of my life with." He shook his head, sadly. "But, I was unfortunately called away." He lowered his voice and made certain we were alone. "The Official Secrets Act makes it impossible to say more."

Naturally, I was intrigued. The Official Secrets Act? Was he a spy? Even spooks must get pensioned off at some point. Shouldn't he have retired some years ago? "Have you been living the secret life all this time?"

He smiled, revealing those wonderful teeth again. "No. Life intruded and I found myself married and living a very different life. But I never forgot Florence. And now, my wife has passed away, and I wondered if it was possible that Florence still remembered me as I remember her."

It was a very romantic story and the man in front of me glanced quickly at my face as though checking that I, too, was swept away by stirring emotions. In fact, I was that most delightful British word, 'gobsmacked.' The Watt sisters were spinsters of indeterminate age. It was easy to imagine they'd sprung fully formed from tea balls and spent their entire lives serving up raisin scones and crustless sandwiches in our little corner of Oxford. To think of either of them having a date, never mind a man carrying the torch for them, was almost more than I could take in.

I said the only thing I could think of. "As far as I know, Florence Watt is next door at the tea shop now. Perhaps she's the one you should ask?"

He nodded, looking relieved. "I thought I'd stop in here and see if her neighbors knew anything that might stop a man from making a fool of himself."

My mind boggled at the possibilities. Miss Watt with a husband and five children? Not even Miss Watt anymore, but Mrs. Somebody-or-other. "No. I imagine she'd be pleased to see an old friend."

He glanced around my shop, crammed as it was with wools, knitting books and magazines, crochet cottons, needles and hooks and all the assorted notions, plus the completed sweaters, shawls and cardigans that hung on the walls or from racks. He looked toward my back room, though I kept that part of the shop curtained off. I used it to hold knitting classes, but in the floor was a trap door used by my downstairs roomies—a nest of knitting-mad vampires.

When I'd first met them, after I moved here from Boston, I was scared they'd eat me. Now that I understood them better, I'd become quite fond of them. Still, I kept that curtain shut during shop hours as my grandmother, the newest vampire and one who suffered from insomnia, had once or twice shown up in the shop during the day.

"This is such a cozy shop, it makes me want to take up knitting."

"You should. It's a very relaxing hobby." I don't know how I kept a straight face, saying things like that. Knitting was a diabolical exercise in frustration. Most everything I tried to knit ended up looking like something from the hedgehog family. Still, it wouldn't look good to admit that the person running a knitting shop couldn't knit, so I'd picked up a few pat phrases. He nodded, still looking around. "You weren't even born when I was last here. Another woman used to run this shop."

"Yes. My grandmother, Agnes Bartlett. She passed away a few months ago. I'm her granddaughter, Lucy."

"I'm sure she'd be very proud to know you're doing such a wonderful job."

"Thank you."

He pulled his shoulders back like a soldier about to go on parade. "Well, Lucy, wish me luck, won't you?"

"Yes, of course. Good luck." As he walked out I saw him glance at his own reflection in the windowpane of the door. I suspected it was insecurity rather than vanity that had him checking his appearance and I found the gesture rather charming.

Naturally, I was dying to discuss this very strange turn of events with my grandmother but, at this time of day, she'd be sound asleep. Fortunately, the vampire knitting club was meeting that night.

She nearly always came up an hour or so before the

meeting so she and I could prepare the back room and have a visit before the others turned up.

I glanced at the big clock on the wall. It was ten-thirty in the morning. I had some time to wait. I wondered if there was anything in my witch's book of spells about moving time forward, then decided against consulting my grimoire. It would be a frivolous use of my newfound powers. Besides, with my luck, I'd push the clock forward fifty years or something instead of a couple of hours. I had only recently discovered I was a witch, and more recently than that, discovered the old grimoire, my family's book of magic spells that had been added to for centuries.

There were spells in there for curing rickets and restoring moonlings, for warding off demons and cursing your enemies. I'd treat the book as harmless fun, like those old cookbooks that tell you how to make jellied calves brains or nettle pudding, except that I'd tried to get the kettle to boil without plugging it in. After memorizing the spell and putting my whole concentration into it, I'd made the kettle explode and put a hole in the ceiling. Magic, I'd discovered, wasn't harmless fun. It was volatile and tricky. Frankly, I was terrified of it. The less I needed to poke around in that old grimoire, the better.

The two things I'd tried that I was the least talented in were knitting and witching; just my luck those were the two occupations in my new life.

My beloved grandmother, who used to be a witch but was recently turned into a vampire, insisted all I needed was practice. Every time I felt the urge to open that grimoire, which wasn't often, I looked up at the new plaster on the kitchen ceiling and reminded myself of how much it had cost to repair.

Turned out, there was no spell to make bills disappear.

Instead of magicking away my time, I spent an hour on the computer putting in an order for woolen supplies. It was quiet in the shop, so I had plenty of leisure to wonder what was going on next door. Had the aged beau met up with Miss Florence Watt? Was their old love even now rekindling?

I had my back to the door and was counting crochet hooks when the bell rang indicating I had a new customer. I didn't need to turn around to know who it was. A chill began at the nape of my neck and traced down my spine like a cold raindrop sliding down a windowpane. I knew it was Rafe Crosyer.

Rafe was also a vampire, but an extremely sexy one. I had a bit of a crush on him, truth to tell, even though he scared me most of the time. He was like a barely-tamed wolf. Magnificent and sleek, but I was never entirely certain he wouldn't revert to a hungry animal at the most inopportune moment.

I dropped the hooks into the basket, immediately forgetting how many I'd just counted and turned to greet the vampire.

He looked tall, cool and elegant as always. His black hair was recently cut and emphasized the chiseled leanness of his cheeks. He wore black woolen trousers with a gray cashmere sweater and over it a tweed jacket. He looked like a particularly sexy Oxford Don, although much younger and better dressed than most of them.

Rafe rarely seemed to sleep. I got the feeling he survived on cat naps. As usual I felt both drawn and repelled by him.

He looked as though something very bad had happened. He stood, silent and staring.

"Can I help you with something?"

"Have you heard the news?"

I don't know how he did it, considering that he tried to keep a low profile, but Rafe always seemed to know everything that was going on, not only in Oxford, but in the world at large. "You mean about Miss Watt?"

His ice blue eyes narrowed on my face. "Miss Watt? What about her?"

I felt mildly pleased. "I know something you don't know. For once." I recounted my meeting with the older gentleman who had come to romance Miss Watt.

His long, fastidious nose wrinkled. "How banal. No, something much more serious is happening."

"What?" I pictured bad vampires coming from another town, a powerful and evil witch come to challenge me to some kind of witch's duel, which I would certainly lose. Plague, pestilence or at the very least a bad weather forecast.

He said, "A toyshop is opening in the next block. You know what that means, don't you?"

"More foot traffic? Increased business?" I tried to be hopeful and look on this new development in an optimistic fashion.

Rafe shook his head at my naïveté. The disdainful look deepened. "Children."

"What's wrong with children?" I'm hoping to have a couple myself one of these days.

"Noisy, destructive little demons." Like vampires were the peaceful sort.

He would've passed through into the back room that led

down to the tunnels below the shop, where most of the local vampires lived. Though I don't know what he was going to do down there, since most of them would be asleep.

I had an idea. I suppose I was as much of a romantic as a woman suffering a recent heartbreak could be, and I was dying to know what was going on next door in the tea shop.

I glanced at my watch. It was five to eleven. My new assistant was due to start work at eleven. "Would you like to go next door and have a cup of tea?"

He glanced at me, oddly. Then I realized that he most likely didn't drink tea. I felt foolish, but before I could say 'never mind' he glanced around. "But, who will look after the shop?"

"Agatha, my new assistant, starts at eleven. Her name is really *Agathe*. She's French."

"Never mind her nationality. Is she a psychopathic liar likely to get herself murdered, like your last assistant?"

Poor Rosemary had indeed been killed and in this very shop. I shuddered at the memory. "That wasn't my fault. Gran hired Rosemary. Anyway, Agatha had excellent references. She worked in a lingerie shop on the Champs Elysees before coming here."

"Good experience. But can she knit?" Since I couldn't seem to grasp the whole knit one purl two thing, it was imperative I hired assistants who were more talented.

"Yes. She went to convent school and the nuns taught her. The only thing is, I think she despises knitting and looks down on women who wear hand-knitted garments."

He looked significantly at the cardigan I was wearing. It had a cream-colored background covered with individual knitted flowers. Daisies, roses and peonies flopped and fluttered down my front in sickly oranges, reds and pinks. A sweet vampire, Mabel, who had been turned during World War II had knit it for me. The vampires in the knitting club all took turns making me things to wear in the shop. It gave them something to do and usually the sweaters, scarves and dresses they knitted me were works of art. But poor Mabel, while a proficient knitter, didn't have the artistic eye of some of the vampires.

When I'd put the sweater on this morning and looked in the mirror, I'd been forcibly reminded of a knitted toilet paper cover.

He picked up a crochet hook I'd dropped on the floor and placed it in the basket. "If you want a cup of tea, why don't you go upstairs to your flat and plug in the kettle?"

First, I hadn't replaced the one that blew up. Second, what was going on next door was bound to be more interesting than my quiet flat. Quickly, I filled him in on the full story of the lovers who'd been separated for half a century and how badly I wanted to see how the reunion had gone. I suppose, in vampire time, a separation of fifty-five years is equivalent to a couple of weeks to humans, but he agreed to accompany me.

Agatha walked in exactly at eleven. She was forty-ish, thin and incredibly chic in a black dress and heels. She wore her dark red hair in a simple bob. Somehow, watching her move, I was convinced she was wearing the fancy lingerie she used to sell.

She took one look at my sweater and said, "*Mon Dieu.*" I couldn't really blame her. She was wearing pure silk lingerie and I was wearing a very large toilet paper cover.

Before I could explain that we were going next door, the

cheerful bell rang as the door opened. I put on my 'how can I help you?' expression and then my smile went natural when I recognized my cousin, Violet Weeks, and her grandmother, Lavinia. They were both witches, but I didn't hold that against them, as I was one myself.

They greeted me with cheek kisses and friendly smiles. Since the two families had been estranged for many years, I wasn't completely sure I trusted them, but they seemed to come in peace. Lavinia carried a package wrapped in pretty flowered paper with a bow on it. Since it wasn't my birthday or any holiday I was aware of, I raised my eyebrows when she presented it to me.

"Open it." When a wrapped gift was in my hands I tended not to argue with orders to open it. I tore through the wrapping, and, when I saw the gift, a tiny sound of mixed pleasure and sorrow escaped me. Nyx, my cat, jumped from her usual spot curled in the basket of wools in the front window, to come and investigate.

The gift was a framed photograph of my grandmother celebrating her fiftieth year running Cardinal Woolsey's. That had been about five years ago and, if possible, she looked even better now. Vampires continue to look the age they were when turned, but become sleek and strong.

"I found the photo in that box of pictures you gave me and I thought how nice it would look in the shop." She'd had it framed and a window was cut into the mat with the words, "Agnes Bartlett, Proprietor of Cardinal Woolsey's Knitting Shop," and the dates of Gran's birth and death. I guessed that the customers who remembered her would enjoy seeing such a nice memorial and, since Gran was still in my life, I wouldn't feel sad when I saw her picture on the wall. I was pretty sure Gran would also be thrilled when she saw it. Since Lavinia knew as well as I did that Gran was still around, I suspected the picture was a peace offering to her sister.

There were hooks all over the shop for hanging displays so it was easy enough to take down a framed photograph of a woman spinning yarn and replace it with the tribute. "Thank you so much," I said. "The customers who knew her will love it."

My witch relatives were clearly planning to stay a while, and I didn't want to invite them to tea with us. It sounded too much like the beginning of a bad joke. *Three witches and a vampire walk into a tea shop...*

Behind us, Rafe and Agathe chatted away in French. It was the most animated I'd seen my new assistant since I'd hired her four days ago. She fluttered her hands while she talked and dropped her voice to tell him some story that made him laugh.

While they were talking, Lavinia also dropped her voice and said, "And how are you getting on with the grimoire?"

There'd been a struggle for ownership of the book of spells not so long ago and since I'd won the book, I didn't want to tell them how confusing and scary I found it.

I pretended to show huge enthusiasm for the ceiling-wrecking, kettle-destroying book. "Great. I'm really working my way through the spells."

"Excellent," said Lavinia, looking at me as though she knew I was lying. "I'm so looking forward to seeing a demonstration."

Rafe, seeing us deep in conversation, must have realized tea was going to be delayed or cancelled, so he purchased a skein of dark purple angora and left the shop by the front door.

A pair of older women came in and Agatha went forward. They showed her the pattern they'd cut out of a women's magazine. It was for a baby's blanket, and was made of blocks all in different colors of wool, with the letters of the alphabet in contrasting colors. "It's for my second grandchild," the woman with the pattern announced proudly.

"Congratulations," Agatha said, sounding bored.

I was going to have to talk to my new assistant about her attitude.

Meanwhile, I changed the subject from spells to Gran, a much safer topic. I told them she'd love to see them and they should come for a visit one evening. I made the date for two weeks hence, determined to learn a spell or two by then. I could make things happen on my own, and was learning to control my inborn powers, but the formal spells were another matter.

Violet said, "Oh, but we'll see you before then. Don't forget the Wiccan pot luck supper Friday evening at the standing stones."

There was a stone circle near Moreton under Wychwood, where their coven met, and Violet was determined to introduce me to her friends. It was part of the run-up to Samhain and that was a big deal, I knew. One of eight important pagan holidays. But I'd only known I was a witch for a few weeks. I wasn't ready to fill my calendar with Wiccan socials.

Was this the real reason they'd stopped in? To remind me about the supper? I'd so far managed to avoid socializing with my fellow witches. I wasn't very good yet—in fact, disastrous might best describe my spell casting abilities.

Besides, running a vampire knitting club twice a week provided all the socializing with colorful characters I could ever want. "I'll do my best to drop by." I had no intention of going.

A trio of young law students walked in. I knew them well. Since they knitted their way through every lecture, they went through a lot of wool. "I'd better go and help them."

"We'll look forward to seeing you Friday," Lavinia said.

"Unless I get a hot date."

They both laughed as though I were hilarious. The girl wearing the knitted toilet roll holder getting a date. That was a knee slapper.

Thing was, I really did want a date with a dishy detective inspector. DI Ian Chisholm had flirted with me and I thought he'd been close to asking me out when my assistant was killed and our relationship turned professional. He was about half a millennium younger than Rafe, so definitely closer in age, and alive, which was nice when a girl was thinking about marriage and kids. Trouble was, there were things I didn't want him to know about me and my undead neighbors.

Also, I wasn't sure if he was really interested in me.

The octogenarian tea shop owner next door was getting more action than I was.

CHAPTER 2

Three days passed before I found time to go next door for tea. Rafe walked in to buy more of the purple wool about two in the afternoon. We weren't very busy, so I suggested we go next door for tea and he agreed so readily I suspected he was as interested as I was in how the romance was going.

I pushed my latest knitting project into a tapestry bag, along with my wallet and phone. Rafe's eyebrows rose. "You're planning to knit over tea?"

"No." I lowered my voice so Agatha wouldn't hear. "But the knitters meet tonight and I want you to unsnarl the mess I made."

"I'll need something much stronger than tea if I'm going to fix your knitting," he said, taking my elbow and ushering me out into the blustery wind. Luckily, we were only going next door since I hadn't put on a coat. My sweater was warm enough. Fortunately, it had been Alfred's turn to knit today's creation and he'd taken his inspiration from the latest fashion knitting magazine I sold in the shop.

The pullover was knitted in cranberry wool with golden leaves drifting down the front. It was so beautiful Agatha hadn't turned up her nose, which was as good as a compliment from my fastidious assistant. With it I wore ankle length black trousers and short brown boots.

When we walked into the tea shop, I could feel the subtle shift in the atmosphere, like a still pond after a stone's been thrown into it, long after the initial splash, the ripples continue to stir the surface.

Of Miss Watt and her long-ago suitor there was no sign. I should have expected that; they could hardly catch up on fifty years and rekindle their romance in the middle of a busy tea shop with tourists and locals sipping tea and munching scones.

Still, I hoped that her sister, Mary, might stop by our table for a little gossip as she usually did when I was here. She was seating an American couple who carried a copy of Rick Steves' Guide to England when we arrived. They were raving about how cute the place was. It really was a quaint and charming room, with an oak-beamed ceiling, windowed alcoves and the original oak floor, attractively scarred from a couple of centuries of use. The décor was the perfect backdrop for afternoon tea. Dainty lace cloths covered every table, with glass over top to keep the laundry down, fresh flowers in glass vases, and around the edges of the dining area large dressers covered with tea pots, many of them antique. Two framed prints showed Victorian ladies in frilly dresses taking tea, one set on a perfect green lawn and the other in an elegant living room.

He saw me looking at the prints. "You still haven't been out to see my collection. Would you like to come Sunday?"

I knew he had an art collection that would rival some galleries and I was fairly certain he let very few people into the secret of its existence. I was intrigued, not only by the idea of seeing Van Gogh's and Rembrandts no one knew had survived, but I was curious to see how he lived.

Sylvia, a gorgeous older vampire who'd been a silent screen star in the 1920s, had told me the house was well worth a visit. She'd made it clear he was bestowing a great honor by inviting me. "Yes. I'd love to."

He nodded, not at all surprised that I'd jumped at the invitation. "I'll pick you up about two."

I had a moment to observe Mary Watt before she saw me, and she looked distressed.

Her color was higher than usual and her mouth set in a straight line. However, when the couple were seated and she saw us she beamed her usual sunny smile. "Why, Lucy, what a pleasant surprise. And, Rafe, we haven't seen you since your excellent talk on illuminated manuscripts at the Bodleian. Come in. I've got a lovely table in a quiet corner."

She led us forward and, as soon as we were seated, said, "I'll send Katya right over. She's our new girl. Polish." Instead of stopping to gossip as I had hoped she would, she bustled off to greet the next customer who, most annoyingly, had arrived right behind us.

"Tea for one, please," she said in a soft, Irish accent. She was about sixty, with once-red hair that was now mostly gray. She wore a green woolen coat, black boots and clutched a well-worn handbag to her chest. I wouldn't have noticed her but for the strong sense of sadness I felt. It enveloped her like a rain-laden dark cloud.

Miss Watt led her to a table across the room but she asked, "Could I sit here?" and indicated a table set for two beside ours. "It's got a bit of a view," she explained, though all I could see was gray sky and the shops across the street. Even those were blocked by the man and woman sitting in the window table.

However, Miss Watt sat the woman there and told her the waitress would be right over.

"No sign of the lovebirds," I whispered to Rafe, searching the room once more. I did see a woman who taught yoga locally. I'd been once or twice to the classes she held in the church hall around the corner, but I'd been so busy lately, what with sleepwalking vampire grandmothers, figuring out how to be a witch without destroying my home, and keeping Nyx fed and sufficiently played with, that I hadn't been back. Her name was Bessie Yang and she was one of the calmest women I knew.

She wore her long black hair in a braid that hung over one shoulder of a blue linen shift. With her was a stylish woman with short blonde hair that curled around her ears. They were deep in conversation.

The two best tables in the bow fronts of the windows were occupied by a very stiff looking man in his seventies with white hair, a bristle of white mustache and a very annoyed look on his face. With him was a downtrodden woman about his own age, no doubt his wife.

At the other window table a group of three women and one man were collecting bags to leave. They all spoke

Spanish and wore lanyards and name badges around their necks.

"You're being rather presumptuous. Perhaps Miss Watt had no interest in the old boy, and sent him on his way."

"Then where is she?" I answered my own question before he could dampen my enthusiasm any further. "They are upstairs in the Miss Watts' private quarters talking about old times. I'm sure of it."

"Perhaps. But I would say her sister isn't much of a fan of this match."

So he'd observed that, too. "Maybe she's jealous. It must be difficult to imagine losing her sister to a man after all these years of the two sisters living and working together. I wonder what she'll do if Florence goes off with him."

"Or the old boy tries to move in here."

"I hadn't thought of that."

At that moment our waitress came up to the table. She was an unremarkable looking young woman in her early twenties. Her hair was lank brown and styled in a sloppy bun at the back of her head. She had a round face, hazel eyes and a mouth that would have been her best feature if it were not currently drooping at the edges, either in boredom or general unhappiness.

"Good afternoon," she said. "What would you like to eat?" Her English was competent though her accent was heavy.

Before I could open my mouth, Rafe spoke to her in a language I could only assume was Polish and ended by treating her to his charming smile. No doubt, he had also seen her unhappiness and sought to put her at her ease by speaking to her in her own language. However, the result was not a happy one.

Her eyes widened and she jumped back as though he'd smacked her. Then, she glanced furtively behind her and said, "I am allowed only to speak in English."

With that she scurried away, without taking our order. I glanced at Rafe and saw him watching the girl with a puzzled frown. "Well that was odd," I said. "Why would Miss Watt care if she speaks Polish to a customer? She made poor Miss Watt sound like a terrible tyrant when she's anything but. What did you say to her?" I couldn't imagine Rafe saying anything rude or suggestive to the waitress.

"I asked her how she's enjoying Oxford."

That seemed harmless enough. "Maybe she doesn't want to be reminded of home?"

"Or she doesn't understand Polish."

I was so surprised I stared. "Why would she lie about being Polish?"

"Any number of reasons," he said, with the air of a man who had seen and experienced several lifetimes of human behavior. Also learned more languages than Berlitz.

I couldn't think what those reasons might be, and watched as the possibly-not-Polish waitress cleared the table the Spaniards had vacated.

She headed back to the kitchen bypassing us and also the Irish lady who was staring hopefully over her closed menu.

Before I could grill Rafe about what he meant, Mary Watt started toward us. She had an amazing ability to keep an eye on every table in the tea shop at once. She brought ice water to the American tourists and then came up. "Has Katya taken your order?"

I didn't want to get the new waitress in trouble. The Miss Watts prized efficiency and, as kind as they were, would fire any waitress who couldn't keep up. For some reason, Rafe speaking to her in Polish had rattled the young woman and I didn't want her to be penalized. "We've only just decided what we want."

She glanced at me sharply as though she didn't believe my little white lie. "Why don't I take your order?"

"I'll have a pot of English breakfast tea and a scone with jam and cream," I said. I might be here out of romantic curiosity, but a delicious scone lathered with strawberry jam and clotted cream was a very nice side benefit.

"Do you want the classic scone or would you like to try the chef's daily special? It's made with lemon and white chocolate and it's really very nice."

I nearly fell off my chair. I'd been coming to Elderflower Tea Shop since I was a little girl. I'd tasted my first scone in this very room and had probably eaten hundreds since. In all that time there had never been a choice of scones. Well, that's not quite true; the Miss Watts offered the classic scone or the classic scone with raisins. They never even strayed as far as a cheese scone, and here they were venturing into lemon and white chocolate territory?

To come into the Elderflower Tea Shop and find, not only that one of the Miss Watts had a gentleman caller, but that they were branching out into unfamiliar scone territory was like finding out the earth had begun rotating in the opposite direction. Still, I am not one to look a gift scone in the mouth and so I happily chose the white chocolate and lemon.

Rafe said he'd join me with English breakfast tea. He declined food saying he'd eaten a big lunch.

I felt guilt stricken. When Mary Watt was busy taking the Irish woman's order, I leaned forward. "I'm sorry, I never thought that you probably don't drink tea." I was fairly sure they didn't serve human blood at the tea shop, though after adding white chocolate and lemon scones to the menu, who knew what might turn up next?

"It's fine," he assured me. "One becomes accustomed to blending in."

It wasn't long before Katya returned to our table carrying a tray. On it was one of the Brown Betty teapots and two of the pretty mismatched china teacups the Miss Watts serve tea in. A sandwich plate in another pattern held my scone. A tiny dish of bright red jam and another of clotted cream accompanied this treat.

I understood then why Rafe had chosen the same type of tea as I was having. With one pot between us it would escape notice that he wasn't drinking any. While the young woman was still there I asked him if he wanted ice water, thinking perhaps something cold would be preferable but he declined.

Katya refused to look anywhere near Rafe, presumably in case he broke into another stream of Polish. She placed a pot of tea at the next table and headed back to the kitchen rapidly.

Rafe watched her with a tiny frown. I said, "Maybe you have a terrible Polish accent. Or you speak Medieval Polish or she really is nervous to speak anything but English in the tea shop."

"Perhaps." He did not look convinced.

I was busily spreading cream and jam on my scone while the tea steeped. When I had finished doing that I added milk and sugar to my cup and lifted the teapot. I raised my brows to him in a questioning look. "Shall I pour you some tea?"

"Just half a cup if you would."

I did and then poured the fragrant brew into my own cup. Apart from the grossness of having to rely on drinking blood to stay alive, it must be so sad not to enjoy all the flavors of good food. I bit into my scone, enjoying the thick texture of the cream and the gushy sweetness of the jam and then the flaky texture of the scone. He watched me closely, I thought with envy.

I would've moaned with pleasure at this amazing afternoon treat, but I thought that would be rude.

He waited until I'd swallowed my first bite and taken a sip of tea and then, looking slightly amused, asked, "And is it as good as the classic scone?"

"Oh, yes. They must have a new cook. Florence always does the cooking, but if she's otherwise engaged, maybe they've hired someone new."

As much as I was enjoying the scone, my real purpose in coming here had been nosiness. I wanted to know if that gallant older gentleman had prospered in his errand. The elder Miss Watt was either too busy to come by my table and gossip, or she simply didn't want to talk about her sister's surprise visitor. If it was a shock for her sister to have an old boyfriend turn up, it must have been a shock for her, too.

Now that I looked around me, I saw that not only were the scones changing but so was the regular menu. For as long as I could remember, and that was nearly two decades, the menu had rarely changed. There was quiche of the day, to be sure, but anyone who came here regularly knew the daily quiche was broccoli and Stilton on Tuesday and Wednesday, quiche Lorraine on Thursday and Friday, salmon Saturday and Sunday and on Monday the shop was closed.

Also on the menu was a ploughman's lunch, a never

changing selection of sandwiches and two kinds of salad. Frankly, it was part of the charm of the tea shop that nothing ever changed, and now I was staring at a chalkboard that promised prawn crepes and, even more shocking, a quinoa salad. I would have sworn the Miss Watts wouldn't know what quinoa was.

As I looked around I noticed that several people were partaking of the specials. Of course, they were mostly tourists and outsiders, but still, this entrepreneurial branching into new menu items seemed to be as successful as it was startling. When Miss Watt came within speaking range, I said, "I see you have some new items on the menu. And they seem to be quite popular."

Miss Watt's lips pressed together, causing tiny wrinkles to sunburst around her mouth. "It's that young fellow in the kitchen," she said. "As bold as brass, he tells me our menu's too old-fashioned and if I let him he could make the food service more profitable."

She shook her head. "Whoever heard of quinoa salad in a tea shop? To tell you the honest truth I didn't even know how to pronounce it. Chef had to tell me. But, the world is changing too fast, and now food and people travel all over the globe so you don't know where you are." She leaned close and said conspiratorially, "I blame the internet."

I nodded gravely and decided not to order the prawn crêpe next time I came in as I had intended in order to show solidarity. "Well, at least the new chef is interested in profits. That must be nice."

"I only hope he can make enough extra to pay for his salary. In the old days, Florence and I used to run this place ourselves. Now—" I waited as she fought an internal struggle and then, as though she couldn't keep her feelings bottled up another second, she said, "She's too busy with her fancy man to give proper care and attention to the shop."

I love a good gossip is much as the next woman and, more importantly, I knew that Gran would grill me for information when I got home. One of the things my grandmother found so difficult about being undead was still being interested in the everyday comings and goings of her friends and neighbors without being able to show herself. So, I was able to indulge in a good gossip and still pretend virtuously that I was only doing it for Gran. "It sounds like you don't like him very much."

Her gaze met mine and her normally placid blue gaze sharpened into what looked like fury. Once more, she pressed her lips together as though to hold back the words she longed to say and then finally managed, "He makes her happy. I suppose that's what really matters."

"It must be nice to have the extra help, not only in the kitchen, but out front." I motioned toward the Polish girl who was balancing a tray rather precariously as she walked toward a table by the window where a stiff, military-looking older gentleman watched her through hard eyes. With him was a nervous-looking woman who was speaking softly to the man.

Miss Watt didn't look particularly thrilled with her new hire. "They arrived together. Asked was I hiring? He'd been a cook first in Poland and then in Prague and Paris. Well, Florence was out with her *friend* until all hours. I had all the cooking to do and the front of house to manage. I couldn't do it all.

Florence's beau had come into my shop only four days ago. A lot had happened in a short time.

"That young man came to talk to me as I was at my wit's end. He said, 'let me help you today, and my sister Katya will waitress out front, and if you don't like what we can do, you don't have to pay us.'"

"Like a free trial," I said. Smart.

"I was so desperate that I said yes. And, to give him credit, he makes a lovely scone. If only he didn't insist on these new-fangled foods. Still, people seem to like them."

"A brother and sister team? That's unusual."

She nodded, glanced at Katya who looked around, as though she was lost. "Oh he's been a chef all right and he's well-trained, but if that girl's ever waitressed before, I'm the Queen of Sheba."

I had to admit, she did seem a bit clumsy. "Maybe she's just nervous."

"Perhaps. Anyway, I need the help, and these days beggars can't be choosers." She'd been watching the progress of Katya on the tray and suddenly stepped toward the waitress. "No, Katya, not that one. You want table number four."

The poor girl looked completely confused and stood in the middle of the room glancing around. Miss Watt shook her head and, almost under her breath, said, "She's getting all the table numbers wrong. It's hopeless." And then she left us and in a low voice directed the new waitress to the correct table.

Rafe and I chatted as I finished off my scone and poured a second cup of tea. I was disappointed not to see Florence, but at least I now knew that she hadn't sent her lost love packing and that Mary wasn't a fan of the match.

I felt a sudden prickling in my fingertips, like a mild electric shock, and I looked over to see that Katya had returned from the kitchen with an overloaded tray. She was looking around the room and I could see her lips moving as she counted tables.

A sharp word from Miss Watt startled her. I watched the tray wobble, as though in slow motion, and I knew it would fall and everything on it would smash if I didn't do something fast.

I focused my attention on the tray, on the cups, on the large teapot that was even now beginning to slide. *Hold steady*, I said under my breath and to my absolute shock the tray obeyed me. Even as Katya's mouth opened in an O of horror, she'd regained control of her burden. I felt a glow of triumph—I had taken on gravity and won.

Rafe was watching me from across the table and he said, in a low voice, "Well done."

The vampire saw altogether too much, but there was no point pretending I hadn't done what he had so clearly seen me do. "I think it was beginner's luck." I kept my gaze on Katya in case she needed my help again, but she managed to unload her tray without disaster. "Honestly, I'm a useless witch. I can't get any of the spells in the grimoire to come out right. I have no idea why I was able to get it right this time."

"You had success because your emotions were involved. You genuinely wanted to save that woman from breaking the crockery and probably being fired."

No doubt he was right, still, I was pleased to see I could do a simple spell if I had to.

"I wish Miss Watt and her boyfriend were here. Her sister obviously doesn't approve, and I want to see for myself whether he's good for her or not." I took a sip of my tea. "Actually, I know Gran will be full of questions and I want her to feel as though she'd been here herself."

He nodded and, looking down, ran the tip of his index finger along the rim of the saucer underneath his untouched tea. "We need to talk about your grandmother."

My stomach clenched at the words. "Why? Everything's all right, isn't it?" I'd already lost Gran once. I didn't want to lose her again.

"Agnes is adjusting fairly well, but it's not good for her to remain too connected with daywalkers." That would be me. "Under normal circumstances I would suggest your grand-mother move away. That's what most of us do when we first get turned. It's difficult to stay in the same neighborhood where you daren't be seen or recognized. Of course, after a generation or two have passed, we can return to our homes. No one recognizes us anymore."

I felt coldness in my chest as though my heart had frozen. "You can't send Gran away." Even though what he said made sense, I couldn't imagine losing her again. Our relationship wasn't always easy, since she was undead and trying to teach me how to be a witch, but I loved her and I still needed her. As well as witch lessons, she gave me good advice on running the shop.

He regarded me steadily. "It's not my decision. I can help her, but she must decide her own future."

I put my thumbnail to my mouth, a habit I have when I'm nervous. "You think I'm being selfish, keeping her here. I can understand that it would be easier for Gran to go somewhere else as she becomes accustomed to her new reality. But I'd miss her so much." I felt almost panic stricken at the thought of running the shop and dealing with my witchy relatives without Gran, but I wanted to do the right thing. "Have you talked to her about moving?"

His smile was rueful. "She won't hear of it. So long as she feels you need her, she'll stay."

I was relieved, of course, but I also felt guilty. "Maybe we should both go somewhere else. If we could find someone sympathetic to run the knitting shop—"

I was about to say more but I glanced towards the entrance and felt my eyes widen. Miss Watt and her boyfriend were just entering the shop, not a minute after I had voiced a wish to see them here. Rafe, followed my gaze. When I looked back at him I said, "I'm on fire today. I wished for them and here they are."

He appeared unconvinced. "I think that might have been coincidence."

I pulled down my mouth in a pout. "Party pooper." He probably didn't know what the term meant, but before he could question me or I elaborate, Miss Watt had seen me and come forward to our table.

CHAPTER 3

"*L*ucy, how lovely to see you."

She was the one who looked lovely. She appeared at least ten years younger than her normal age, was wearing makeup and, I think, a new dress. She'd definitely had her hair done in a much more modern style and her normally gray hair was now an age-defying ash blond.

A lot had happened around here in a few days.

"It's nice to see you, too."

"And I believe you've met Gerald Pettigrew?"

"Yes."

The old man grinned at me in a cheeky fashion. "You're the young woman from next door." He turned to Florence. "Lucy encouraged me to be bold enough to seek you out." Not entirely true, but nice that he'd given me matchmaking credit.

She then introduced him to Rafe and the two men shook hands. She glowed with happiness and he glowed with pride.

It was nice to see this golden age romance taking off, and I felt a personal interest in the outcome. I hadn't made the match but I felt that in my small way I had helped it along.

"You must have been surprised to see Mr. Pettigrew again, after so long."

She put a hand to her heart—she'd sprung for a manicure, too, and her nails were a soft pink and shaped like ten perfect candied almonds. "I can't describe what it was like. He walked into the kitchen and surprised me with my hands covered in flour, my hair a mess—"

"You looked beautiful. Exactly as I remembered you," he said, reaching for her hand.

"It was such a shock," she continued, "but a lovely one. I felt as though the years fell away and I was young again."

"I'm a much older man, but I hope a wiser one." He winked at me. "I won't be letting her out of my sight a second time. And—" He wagged his index finger at me. "You must call me Gerald."

"I'm so happy," Florence said simply. Not that she needed to say the words; she absolutely glowed with happiness.

"I was afraid you wouldn't even recognize me," Gerald said. "The years haven't always been kind."

She smiled up at him. "You look older, yes, but I knew you instantly. I'd have known you anywhere."

"And I, you."

They stood by our table for a couple of minutes chatting about how they'd been going back to their old haunts and seeing things through new eyes. "Of course, things haven't changed in some ways, but there was no Harry Potter fifty years ago. Christ Church College was just a college. Now? The place is overrun with tourists wanting photos of the

Hogwarts dining room." He threw up his hands in mock outrage. "I ask you."

She put her hand on his arm when she described their outing to the Perch, a riverside pub where they had enjoyed their first date half a century earlier. He rested a hand on her shoulder as he said, "The pub's changed a bit, but you, my dear, haven't changed at all."

She shook her head and blushed, then giggled. A very odd sound coming from this woman I had been certain was a confirmed spinster.

It seemed as though they couldn't bear not to be connected in some physical way. If one didn't have their hand touching the other they stood so close that their arms brushed and they shared each other's personal space. Miss Watt told Gerald that Rafe was an expert in old book restoration. Gerald shook his head. "Everyone in Oxford is so clever. I always feel such a dreadful fool when I come here." He pointed to his own head. "Thick as two short planks."

"Nonsense," Florence Watt cried. "You're as clever as anyone. You're very intelligent just not an intellectual." Then she beamed at us. "I told Gerald I'd take a busman's holiday today and treat us to the full cream tea. I can't remember the last time I acted like a customer in my own tea shop. Probably never."

The other Miss Watt had been keeping us in her peripheral vision. As the two lovebirds turned away from our table she came up. "Joining us for tea?" she asked in a shrill, over-friendly tone, as though they were tourists down from Manchester. Her sister looked taken aback and said, "Yes. If it's convenient?"

There was an edge to her voice. My instinct had been

right that her sister wasn't entirely happy with this love match.

"Of course." She made to lead them toward an empty table beside the wall but her sister stopped her and said, "We'd like table six."

I saw her sister pinch her lips together. If Gerald Pettigrew's return had taken ten years off Florence, it seemed they'd been handed off to Mary. Her hair looked grayer, her complexion more colorless and a general air of trouble seemed to hang about her. "As you wish."

"And there's no need to escort us there. I know my way around the tea shop."

Her sister turned on her heel and stalked back into the kitchen. I suspected she disapproved of her sister acting like a customer and certainly one taking one of the best tables during a busy time. I also doubted that Mary had ever taken a busman's holiday and sat down to an afternoon tea.

The two lovers made their way to the recently vacated table by the window. Two bright spots of color burned on Miss Watt's cheekbones and she muttered something to her partner who reached out a hand and placed it over hers reassuringly. Immediately, her color ebbed and her smiles returned.

I imagine I imitated her posture as I leaned in towards Rafe and said in a low voice, "I'd say there's trouble in paradise."

"Definitely an old fox in the hen house."

A moment later Katya crossed the room with her heavy tread and her notebook. Miss Watt ordered the champagne afternoon tea for the pair of them. "I'll have the English breakfast tea with it."

"And for you, sir?" Katya asked Gerald Pettigrew.

"A pot of Earl Grey for me, if you please."

Katya hadn't yet learned the trick of constantly scanning the tea shop. Where the owner would have offered fresh hot water to one table, removed an empty plate from another and always been on the lookout for any hint that she was needed, Katya turned and headed straight for the kitchen with her order, oblivious to the fact that the old man in the other window table was red-faced and beckoning to her. Finally, he barked, "Girl, I say, waitress," in a commanding and irritated tone. He sounded as though he might once have been a military man. Katya certainly sprang to attention at his tone. I think we all did.

She turned toward his table and he said, "You've brought me the wrong tea. I don't know what this muck is but I ordered Earl Grey. This is some sort of fruit tea and you can take away this honey, I'll have proper milk and sugar."

"Very sorry, sir," she said, and picked up the pot and his cup. Bessie Yang, the yoga teacher, said, "I think that was my tea, my dear. That's all right. You can leave that pot with me, and the honey. I've got a cup here."

Poor Katya was beginning to look quite bewildered. She dropped the pot of tea and the honey with the yoga teacher who said gently, "And the quinoa salad when you get a moment."

The waitress smiled at her in gratitude and promised to check with the kitchen and then walked swiftly out of the room. The old man watched her go with a frown pulling his white brows together. His mustache bristled to attention when he spoke to the mousy woman I assumed was his wife. "Foreigners!"

Rafe leaned in and said, "And to think I imagined afternoon tea would be a dull affair."

"We'll have so much to tell Gran. I'll just run to the loo and then I'd like another cup of tea if that's all right with you."

"I have no pressing engagements."

I'd never thought much about vampires before moving to Oxford. But now that I'd met Rafe and the other members of the vampire knitting club I sympathized with being doomed to walk the earth forever, always in the shadows, an animal of prey, terrifying to the race of humans to which they used to belong. At least modern vampires had blood banks and other ways to get the blood they needed, and, thanks to the rise in skin cancer, modern technology had invented all sorts of fabrics to keep sun off the body. It must be much nicer being a vampire now than in the past, but I still thought it was melancholy to have to plan a future that had no end.

I excused myself and went upstairs to where the bathrooms were. I had to pass Mary Watt and I thought she'd been crying. She looked far from well. "Miss Watt, are you all right?"

She jumped when I spoke. "Oh, I was miles away. Just feeling my age, really. Running Elderflower is too much for one person, I'll have to think about retiring. It's impossible to find decent help and I can't manage on my own."

I made a sympathetic noise. She was obviously stressed about her sister's rekindled love affair and what it might mean for their future. She pulled a handkerchief from beneath her sweater cuff and wiped her eyes. "Look at them. My sister's completely lost her head over that silly man. She's certainly stopped doing anything useful since he arrived.

Well, if she wants to be a customer at Elderflower, perhaps it should belong to someone else." Her logic was a little garbled but I understood the sentiment.

"I'm sure once the initial excitement of seeing him again passes, she'll return to her usual, industrious self." I had no idea if this was true but I wanted to comfort Mary Watt.

She made a rude noise. "Oh you do, do you? Well, I can tell you, she was just as mad over that man fifty years ago and if I hadn't..." She shook her head and tucked her hankie away. "Well, it was years ago, I'm sure you're right. Everything will be fine. I must get back."

When I returned to the table, Miss Watt was seating a group of four ladies who were telling her that they'd all been at school together, at St. Hilda's. They all looked to be in their seventies. One was glamorous with stylish blonde hair, trendy glasses and wearing a smart black suit. The other three had given up on style, if they'd ever bothered with it. Their hair was gray, they didn't appear to be wearing makeup and their clothes were designed for comfort rather than style. Mary smiled, as though she hadn't a trouble in the world, and said with a twinkle, "Hildabeasts." The ladies all laughed merrily. "Yes, indeed. Of course, that was in the days when there were only two colleges open to women. We were glad to get places."

"And you're here for a reunion?"

They sobered immediately. The blonde smiled sadly and wiped at the corner of her eye with the back of her hand. "A funeral. We've reached the age when we only see each other when one of our friends passes away."

"Oh, I am sorry," said Miss Watt. "May I start with you with a nice pot of tea?"

The blonde one who seemed to be their unofficial spokesperson said, "Oh, I think a sherry to begin with. Something to brace us up before we have our tea." She glanced around, "Unless you prefer something else?" They all agreed on sherry.

"Of course."

Miss Watt went to the back of the room where the drinks were kept, passing Katya, carrying a heavy tray. She headed for the grumpy man who'd complained. "Here's your Earl Grey tea."

As she plunked it on his table, he glared at her. "About time too. I imagine it's cold by now. And I've already finished my scone."

She mumbled something that could have been sorry or could've been a Polish curse and then took her wobbling tray to Florence Watt and Gerald Pettigrew. I kept a steady eye on the tray but no magical intervention was needed and she managed to put the three-tiered tray of sandwiches, scones and tiny pastries onto Miss Watt's table along with the two pots of tea, and two flutes of champagne without further mishap.

Florence Watt removed the lid of her teapot then wrinkled her nose and shook her head. She replaced the lid and exchanged her teapot with Gerald's. I watched her go through the same routine and nod, then pour her tea.

Mary Watt arrived with the sherry and placed four glasses in front of the four ladies from St. Hilda's. The four women toasted their departed friend and, as they sipped and chatted, they reminded me of my grandmother and her friends. I still wasn't used to her being gone-but-not-gone. How much harder must it be for her? Perhaps Rafe was right and we should move somewhere else, so she could go out in public. At least until she got used to her new life.

Rafe broke into my thoughts. "Your grandmother will make the transition, but it takes some time."

My gaze jerked back to his. "Do you read minds?"

He looked amused. "One doesn't need to be a mind reader with you, Lucy. Your face is so expressive."

I felt a little foolish. "I've got no poker face, that's for sure."

"Also nothing to hide, which is very refreshing. Most of us spend too much time and energy trying to conceal our thoughts."

He looked melancholy but I didn't pry. I suspected it was better for me if he did conceal, not only his thoughts, but his past.

The grumpy military looking man called across the room to Miss Watt for his bill. On hearing his voice, the blonde of the four ladies turned toward him. "Why Colonel Montague. How very nice to see you."

When he saw who was addressing him, his peevish expression relaxed. "Miss Everly. Come back to your old haunts, I see."

She laughed in a coquettish manner and rose and went over to chat with him and his wife for a minute or two. The wife put on a polite smile but it was the colonel who looked pleased, and his irate manner changed so fast it was like sunshine succeeding a storm.

Miss Watt brought over his bill and he continued to chat with Miss Everly. Under the gray afternoon light coming through the window, I thought he grew red in the face.

Maybe he was embarrassed, or perhaps felt foolish chatting up another woman in front of his wife.

Miss Everly returned to her table.

Florence and Gerald, meanwhile, had finished their champagne and had barely touched their sandwiches and cakes. They seemed more interested in each other than the food.

Someone began to cough. I barely noted it, thinking about Florence and Gerald, when the coughing grew worse. It was the grumpy man in the window. "Excuse me," he managed, coughing and coughing, growing increasingly red in the face.

Conversation petered out as the dreadful racking coughing continued.

Miss Everly jumped to her feet and called in a loud, sharp voice, "Water. Bring him some water."

He waved her away as she went forward but she ignored his protests and thumped him on the back. "Are you choking?" she shouted over the sound of his cough.

He shook his head, and pushed up to his feet.

Florence Watt had jumped up from her tea table at Miss Everly's command and ran to the back of the room where a jug of water and glasses was kept. Rapidly, she filled a glass and rushed forward.

The colonel grabbed his neck with both his hands. I've never actually seen anyone froth at the mouth, but that's what he was doing.

"Teddy!" his wife cried, leaping to her feet.

"He's choking," Miss Everly said. "I shall try the Heimlich maneuver."

I had that helpless feeling of wanting to do something but

having no idea what. I began to rise, thinking perhaps I might loosen his collar, when Rafe put his hand over mine. "Leave him be. There's nothing to be done for him, now."

Miss Everly got her fisted hands underneath his diaphragm and pulled up with impressive energy. Air was expelled along with bubbles. Then the man sagged to the floor, taking Miss Everly with him.

Bessie Yang said something to her table companion and the woman rose, looking somewhat reluctant. She walked over to where the colonel was gasping and flailing. "If you could all step back. I'm a doctor." At that moment she looked as though she wished she had passed on medical school so she could have been allowed to drink her tea in peace. The man's wife cried, "Teddy, what's wrong?"

The doctor said to Miss Everly, who'd struggled to her knees, "Help me roll him onto his side." To the wife she said, "Is he epileptic?"

"No, there's never been anything like that in our family."

"Heart condition?"

The wife was beginning to cry, wringing her hands. "Quickly, does he have a medical condition I should know about?"

"No. He had a stroke last year, but the doctor said it was mild."

"Call an ambulance," the doctor ordered. She was unbuttoning his shirt as she spoke. I couldn't see what she did, then, but the colonel grew quieter.

His wife, meanwhile, seemed to have trouble comprehending what was happening. "He takes pills, for his blood pressure. Otherwise he's in excellent health."

The doctor looked at her with pity. She shielded him

from view, but we could see him curled into himself. "I must tell you, your husband is seriously ill."

Rafe leaned toward me. "In fact, he's dead."

WITHIN SEVERAL MINUTES it was clear that Rafe had spoken the truth. The man's coughing and thrashing stopped. He lay quiet and still. It was unnaturally quiet in the tea room after all the commotion. All eyes were turned his way.

Several customers had risen from their seats but no one seemed to know what to do. The doctor turned to the worried looking wife and said, "I'm very sorry but your husband is gone."

"Gone? But he's right there."

"He's dead. I'm so sorry."

The woman stared for a moment and her face went bright red and then deathly pale and she began to sob. Miss Everly rose and pulled her seat closer to the sobbing woman. She glanced around, "Mary? Might we have another sherry here?"

"Do you know the doctor?" I asked. Rafe usually knew everyone.

"Only by sight. Dr. Amanda Silvester. She works out of a clinic on Mansfield Street."

Gerald Pettigrew stood up, leaving most of the afternoon tea intact. "Well, what a tragic event. I think the best thing to do is to leave this poor man in peace." Florence seemed uncertain as to whether she should go with him or stand by her sister. Dr. Silvester shook her head at him. "No one must leave this place. Not until the police have arrived."

He puffed up his chest as though about to argue, when Florence Watt cried, "Police?"

The doctor rose to her feet. "I'm afraid so. We'll have to do a post mortem of course, but I believe this man was poisoned."

The two Miss Watts turned to stare at each other and then instinctively closed ranks until they were standing side-by-side. Mary Watt said, "Poisoned? But we have an excellent hygiene rating and our baking is fresh every day. I'm sure you must be mistaken. His wife said he takes pills for his heart."

The doctor looked at her with sympathy but clearly had no intention of getting into an argument with the tea shop owner about how this man had died. She simply repeated that she wouldn't know for certain until a post mortem had been conducted.

It was absolutely awful after that. There was a dead man lying in the middle of the tea shop like the proverbial elephant in the middle of the room. I'd have given anything to have an actual elephant standing there not a man who had died violently in front of my eyes. I looked at Rafe. "Do you think he was poisoned?"

He nodded.

I couldn't get my head around it. "You mean on purpose?"

"That would be my guess."

"That would mean he was—"

"Murdered. Yes, I believe he was."

I felt hot and cold chills running up and down my skin. People began to talk amongst themselves in low voices and over all of it could be heard the painful sound of a new widow's sobs.

CHAPTER 4

*I*t was a relief when the police arrived. Detective Inspector Ian Chisholm caught my eye first. I had never seen him look so serious. With him was an older, heavyset man who was obviously in charge. They both paused at the tea shop entrance and I thought each took a mental photograph of the crime scene.

As Ian's eyes swept over the crowd he saw me. His eyes lightened for a moment, crinkling at the corners and he gave an infinitesimal nod. I felt better immediately knowing he was here. The older man said in a commanding tone, "I'm Detective Chief Inspector Roderick Blake and this is Detective Inspector Ian Chisholm. We'll need statements from each of you, as soon as we can find a suitable location, we'll move you there. In the meantime, please stay where you are."

The American woman cried, "You can't leave us here with the dead man."

A man snapped back, "He can't hurt you."

"Only for a few more minutes, madam, if you wouldn't mind," said the chief inspector.

At that moment, the police photographer arrived along with a tall, thin man who immediately went up to Dr. Silvester. Rafe said, "He's Dr. Fred Gilbert, Forensic Medical Examiner, the police surgeon. She was right to call him in." The two doctors huddled beside the body while the photographer snapped photos, not only of the corpse, but everything on the table. And, after the chief inspector had told us all to resume our seats, exactly as we were sitting when the man died, he photographed the rest of us.

The paramedics loaded the body onto a stretcher and covered him with a sheet. I was pleased for the sake of the widow they hadn't zipped him into a body bag. It would have felt so disrespectful somehow. Though I doubt she'd even have noticed. She was sitting now at the table of the four ladies who'd come here to mourn another friend.

She looked stunned and sat there saying, "I can't believe it. It can't be true. Teddy has his golf trip tomorrow. He's been so looking forward to it." She folded her arms on the table and put her head down and sobbed. As the stretcher was wheeled past I noticed Miss Everly close her eyes and her lips moved in what I assumed was prayer.

The Irish woman raised her hand as the colonel's remains rolled by. Instead of making the sign of the cross as I'd expected, she stuck her middle finger in the air.

"Did you see that?" I whispered to Rafe. "She flipped him the bird."

"I wonder why." As we continued to watch her, the woman turned her back on the corpse as it continued on its way.

I couldn't believe it. "First she gave him the one finger salute and then she turned her back on him. Why would anyone do that?"

"It looks like something your people would do. Curse someone and then shun him."

"My people?" I knew he was referring to witches, not Americans, but I wasn't easy about being a witch. I certainly didn't want to be associated with anyone who would disrespect a dead man like that.

His eyes flickered with humor but he wisely left me to my outrage without commenting further.

The chief inspector told us not to touch or move anything and definitely not to eat or drink what was in front of us. He needn't have worried. Plates of half eaten food, cups filled with tea, all remained untouched. The American woman, who sounded like a New Yorker, said, "I'm starting to feel sick. Do you think it's botulism? Remember when that deli got closed down on forty-first?"

"That was salmonella," her helpful spouse said. "Here, have a mint."

She eyed the packet suspiciously. "You didn't buy them here, did you?"

"No. At the airport." Only then did she take a mint.

ELDERFLOWER BECAME crowded as more police arrived and no customers left. One of the ladies sitting with Miss Everly turned out to be the verger at the church around the corner and had the key to the church hall. We were all politely requested to make our way over to the hall where we'd be interviewed and then allowed to go.

The Irish woman came over as we all rose and headed for the door. "Well, isn't this a terrible thing?" she asked, walking by my side. "To think of the man dropping dead over his tea."

"Did you know him?" Based on her strange behavior, she'd either held a grudge against the colonel, or was giving the finger to death in general.

She hesitated. "No. I never met the man." Okay, maybe she held a grudge against death. The longer I lived in Oxford, among witches and vampires, the less things surprised me.

As we filed out of Elderflower and up the street toward the church we must have looked like a funeral procession. The bay windows of Elderflower looked like eyes bugging out and staring as we walked by. My shop was brightly lit and I longed to be inside it, with all the wools I didn't know how to knit with, patterns I couldn't understand, and an assistant who held me and my shop in contempt.

Harrington Road ended at New Inn Hall Street, where the Methodist Church of St. John sat, as though at the head of a long table, with its graveyard on the left hand side and the church hall on the right. There were many beautiful buildings in Oxford. St. John's church hall was not one of them. A low, gray stone building, it seemed dark and unwelcoming even when Bessie Yang turned on the lights. There were long tables in rows and a sign on the wall inviting parishioners to join the choir. It smelled like dust and mildew.

The chief inspector set himself at a table at the front of the room and asked that we all take a seat. We'd be interviewed and were asked to empty our pockets and purses.

He asked the widow to join him first. She seemed unable

to move, until the kind and capable Miss Everly put her arm around her and supported her.

Then, either Ian or one of the two uniformed officers would join a party at their table, ask questions, and take notes, before moving onto the next one. Rafe and I sat at the end of one of the long tables, waiting for them to get to us. I leaned in and whispered, "It feels like speed dating."

"Like what?" Rafe asked me. Right, I doubt they'd had speed dating back in Shakespeare's time or whenever he'd actually been young.

I might make flippant remarks but I also felt creeped out. "If the colonel was poisoned, his murderer could be in this room." I looked around but everyone appeared so *ordinary*. The four ladies who'd come to mourn their friend. The woman who taught yoga and her doctor friend. Tables of tourists looking bewildered, and poor Gerald Pettigrew who sat, alone now, clearly wishing he were somewhere else.

Florence and Mary stood together not far from us. "This is dreadful," Florence said. "We'll never live it down."

But Mary appeared to be rising to the challenge. "Nonsense. It's an unfortunate incident, but we'll get through it. We've a business to run."

Right. And so did I. "I'd better call Agatha," I said to Rafe. She'd probably have to close up. I took my cell phone to the farthest corner of the hall so as not to disturb the investigation. I told my assistant I might be late and tried to think of a plausible excuse, but she showed no curiosity at all about why I might be absent from the shop, merely said she'd lock the door if I wasn't back by five.

I passed Katya, who was standing near the back of the room. With her was a young man I had never seen before.

They were talking together in low voices. I could only assume he was her brother, the chef. He was a muscular, good-looking guy maybe my age or a little older, say late twenties, of average height. Beneath his short-sleeved T-shirt I could see a tattoo of a dragon on his bicep.

The verger brought in a case of bottled water and passed bottles around while we waited. People looked at their watches or at the round clock on the wall that seemed to hold onto time and then burp it out jerkily. The only one who seemed unconcerned was Rafe, as though he had all the time in the world, which, of course, he did.

It was Ian who came to our table, whether by chance or design I wasn't sure. "I'm sorry such a shocking thing should happen as you were enjoying a cup of tea." No doubt he'd said that to every person he'd interviewed.

"It was awful," I agreed.

He nodded and opened the notebook. "Lucy, I'll start with you. I think I know most of it but let's go through it again for the official record. I need your full name, date of birth, address and contact information. I'm afraid I'll have to ask for official identification."

"Of course," I reached for my purse. I wondered what Rafe would do for ID. He was one who tended to keep to the shadows. Did he have such a mundane thing as a driver's license or passport? He calmly reached into his pocket and pulled out a perfectly modern-looking wallet containing perfectly legitimate looking ID. Our gazes connected and he gave me the ghost of a wink.

After these preliminaries, Ian asked me to describe every-thing I'd seen. "Take your time."

What had I seen? "It was all a bit of a jumble. Let me

think." I tried to think of every detail I remembered. "The man who died, Colonel Montague, was very rude about his tea. That's how I know his name, you see. He called the waitress over, in a very loud voice, because she'd brought him the wrong tea. He wanted Earl Grey and he got the fruit tea that was meant for Bessie Yang, the yoga teacher.

"One of the ladies at the next table recognized his voice and called him by his name. I think her name was Miss Everly. She and her friends were here for a funeral of one of their college chums." I realized I was rambling. It was difficult to focus when my mind kept skipping out on rational thought to "Oh, my God, that old man died right in front of me!" I didn't say that out loud, but the jittery feelings were messing with my concentration.

Ian didn't check me or try to curtail my blathering. He looked at me calmly as though everything I had to say was fascinating and somehow that helped steady me.

Rafe, sitting there so cold and controlled, also helped and I was able to shut out the nervous chatter and question-and-answer interviews going on around me and try to focus on helping the police find out who did this terrible thing.

I took a deep breath and glanced over at Bessie, sitting a couple of tables ahead of us. She was another oasis of calm in the midst of this dreadful experience and I tried to imagine I was in one of her yoga classes, right here on a Tuesday night or a Saturday morning and her calm, low voice was saying, "There is only you and your mat." I closed my eyes and let the scene I had witnessed play like a movie.

"When we came in, the colonel and the woman I assumed was his wife were already seated at the table. Then those four ladies arrived. Miss Florence Watt and her—" I hesitated, looking for the right word, "Her friend arrived soon after that. They stopped at our table and chatted for a few moments. Then they sat at the table in the window."

"The one beside Colonel Montague's."

"That's right. The waitress, Katya, took our order and went back into the kitchen." I had contemplated telling him about the animosity between the two Miss Watts and decided it was irrelevant. "She came back to take Miss Watt and her friend's order and after she did so Colonel Montague called her over to complain that he'd been given the wrong tea. He said it was fruit and he'd ordered—" I stopped myself again. "Sorry. I already told you that."

"It's all right. Better you tell me things twice than leave something out." He was so calm, so reassuring, so nice. I smiled gratefully and went back to my recital.

"Katya took away his tea and the honey, gave it to Bessie and went back to the kitchen. She returned with a new pot of tea for him. He complained that he'd already finished his scone, but he took it anyway."

"You saw him drink the tea?"

I closed my eyes. He'd been in my line of vision, but I wasn't very interested in whether a grumpy old man drank his tea or not. However, as I concentrated I remembered the way he'd been silhouetted against the window. I had definitely seen him. "Yes. I saw him drinking it. He took a sip and then made a face and added more sugar."

I paused, trying to remember things in order. "Then, Katya took a champagne afternoon tea over to Miss Watt and Mr. Pettigrew's table."

"Do you know what kind of tea they had?"

"Florence Watt had English Breakfast and Gerald Pettigrew ordered Earl Grey." I remembered the pantomime of tea sniffing and switching. "They got each other's teas and switched." I sighed. "The new waitress is having trouble remembering which table goes by which number and who ordered what. She's new."

He wasn't writing much down, mostly just listening. I imagine he'd already heard all of this. He asked, "And did you get what you ordered?"

I was happy to tell him that Katya, in our case at least, had made no mistakes and recited our order to him.

"Did you see anyone else go up to Colonel Montague's table?"

"Miss Everly spoke to him. She got out of her seat and they shook hands and then I think she spoke to his wife. But I didn't see anyone else go near the table except Miss Watt who, of course, checks with everyone at least once to make sure they're happy and, I think, brought them their bill. But people do walk around, coming and going, looking for the bathroom."

"Did you see the colonel take any kind of medication?"

I shook my head. "No. But I didn't watch him continuously." I'd been much more interested in the drama playing out between the Miss Watts.

"Did you see what he had to eat?"

"No. As I said, he'd already been served when we got there. It was only the fuss over the tea that made me notice him it all. Though he did say he'd already finished his scone when she finally brought him the correct tea."

"It was definitely the young Polish girl who served him?"

"Yes. Though we're not sure she is Polish."

"I beg your pardon?"

I told him how peculiar she had acted when Rafe spoke Polish to her.

Ian glanced between the two of us. He turned to Rafe, who looked resigned and slightly bored. "You speak Polish?"

"Yes. Not like a native, perhaps, but well enough to get by." Ian was still looking at him curiously and the vampire said, "I have an interest in languages. And, of course, it helps in my work."

Ian looked over to where Katya and her brother stood together in a corner drinking bottled water. A uniformed cop stood with them and Ian caught his eye and beckoned him over. He asked the constable to bring Katya to our table, and, after glancing at Rafe, she spoke in a low voice to her brother. He nodded and they both came to our table.

The girl looked sullen and, I thought, scared, while her brother walked with bravado. He reminded me of the muscle builders in my gym back home in Boston who swaggered around with bowlegged insouciance, lifting the heaviest weights they could while looking at themselves in the mirror. I understood it was for checking their form, but I've always suspected a deep streak of narcissism in the practice.

The pair sat down as Ian directed them to, across the table from each other. He shifted around so he had a clear view of both their faces. He told them he'd need to take their full names and addresses and would like to see official identification.

The two shared a glance and the brother said, "We did not bring any with us. It is in the flat." His accent was as heavy as Katya's. For a brother and sister, they didn't look much alike. He was much better looking than she was, with big gray-blue eyes fringed with dark, curly lashes that any woman would kill for, rugged bone structure and a full-lipped mouth. When he saw me studying him, he smiled at me. Even his teeth were good. Big and white as though he'd happily take a bite out of me. His cheeky grin suggested I'd enjoy it.

"Someone will escort you home later and we'll get it then. Now, I understand you're from Poland?"

Once more that furtive glance that they shared and they both nodded. Katya began to fidget with her hands, rubbing her thumb over her nails, back and forth like she was going to buff them to a shine. "Whereabouts in Poland?"

"Kraków."

Ian said, "I've never been there. I hear it's beautiful."

"Yeah, real nice."

"And what brings you here?"

He shrugged. "Better opportunities."

Katya glanced sideways at Rafe once and then dropped her gaze to the table.

Ian said, "I believe you know Kraków quite well, Mr. Crosyer."

The chef's Adam's apple jumped as he swallowed. "I have not been there in some years."

Rafe smiled. I wondered if that was the smile he gave his victims before he bit them in the neck. I began to feel somewhat sorry for Katya and her brother. "It's not a city that changes overly much, however. Which neighborhood are you from?"

The young man hesitated and then said, "The eastern part."

Rafe nodded. "Volzhskiy or Nie mówię po polsku?"

He must know he was sinking fast, but the brother was

game to the end. He rubbed the back of his neck. "The second one."

And then, of course, as had been inevitable from the beginning, Rafe began to speak to him in Polish.

Beside me, the girl cursed, low and under her breath, but it was a very Anglo-Saxon word—not a hint of a Polish accent to be heard.

Her brother replied, "You speak Polish very well, but my sister and I prefer to speak English in this country."

Rafe appeared to have finished toying with his prey. He smiled and settled back in his chair. "Volzhskiy is in Russia, near Volgograd. The second neighborhood I mentioned is actually a phrase that means, 'I do not speak Polish.'"

Ian took over then and leaned in, looking tougher than I'd ever seen him. I hadn't known he could do bad cop, but he did it well. "Why don't you stop wasting my time and tell me who you really are and where you're from?"

The girl beside me said, "Oh, just tell them, Jim. They know we're not Poles so there's no point pretending." She spoke with an Australian accent and seemed startlingly different when speaking naturally. Her entire face underwent a change and her voice was higher pitched and more pleasant.

The man she called Jim shrugged and opened his hands. He leaned back, retrieving his former bravado. He cracked a grin. "All right. It was a bit of a lark. We're actors, you see. Wondered if we could take on a couple of roles and stay in character, not for a couple of hours a night on stage, but twenty-four-seven. It was working."

"Until a man was murdered. After eating food that you prepared."

Jim leaned in toward Ian and banged his index finger on the table. "I didn't kill that old geezer. Why would I?"

The detective turned to Katya. "What's your real name?"

"Katherine Ainsley. But everyone calls me Katie. We kept our stage names close to our real names to make it easier for us."

"Katie. You were the one who took all the food and tea out to that table. You and Jim had the most access and opportunities to poison Colonel Montague."

Her eyes widened in fright and she glanced at me as though I might be able to help her. "We didn't hurt anyone. He was a rude old git, and I might've given him a scone I'd dropped on the floor, but I wouldn't kill him. Why would I?" Jim had asked the same rhetorical question but this time, Ian answered.

"Perhaps you were acting the parts of murderers? To see if you could get away with it, like being Polish."

Katie shook her head so vehemently I was worried she'd do herself an injury. "I wouldn't do something like that. Never."

Jim took her hand and said to Ian. "Look, mate. I told you. It was for a laugh. We weren't hurting anyone. We wouldn't."

Ian let the silence get thick. "So, you acted being Polish, did you also pretend to be a professional cook?"

"No. I paid for acting school working in restaurants. I know how to cook and I can certainly do it without poisoning the punters."

Ian said, "We'll need a list of places you worked." He turned to Katie. "And did you put yourself through acting school working in restaurants?"

"No I didn't." She was back to being sullen. "It's terrible

work. I'd never do this again. In fact, I told Jim I was going to quit. The work's backbreaking. The old ladies are nice enough, but they're demanding too. The fun's gone out of it. I was planning to quit and find another job."

I could smell Katie's sweat. She was terrified. She swallowed noisily. "And we're not brother and sister. Jim's my boyfriend."

Ian asked, "Have either of you been in trouble with the law?" The pair glanced at each other. "We'll find out easily enough so better to be honest now."

"No." Katie said.

"Jim?"

He shifted in his chair. I could see his knee bobbing up and down like he was keeping time to a very fast song. "Did some time in juvie," he admitted at last. He put on a posh accent and said, "Got in with the wrong crowd."

Ian sent them off with a uniformed constable. First, they were to be escorted to wherever they lived, their ID fetched, and then to the station where they'd be fingerprinted and interviewed further. "Oh, and you'll have to surrender your passports."

"What?" Katie said, looking indignant. "But we haven't done anything."

"Until we prove that's true, we don't want you getting on a plane and heading back to Sydney."

"Melbourne," Jim snapped. "I'll call my lawyer. And the consulate."

"Polish or Australian?" Rafe asked smoothly.

Before Jim could snarl whatever answer was forming in his Neanderthal brain, Ian said, "You're welcome to call anyone you like."

When the pair had left, I asked Ian, "Do you really think one of them killed the colonel?"

I thought he'd brush off my inappropriate question, but he watched them go, frowning. "I don't know. They had the most access to the food. But what connection could there be between two actors from Melbourne, Australia, and a retired colonel from Oxford?"

I'd been thinking. "I wonder if he was even the intended victim."

Both men stared at me and I elaborated. "That poor girl is the most terrible waitress I've ever seen. She kept sending the wrong orders to the wrong tables. Colonel Montague could be dead simply because she mistook table two for table seven."

"Which means," Rafe said, "the intended victim could be anyone in this room."

CHAPTER 5

*J*an picked his notebook up and stood. "If you wouldn't mind going to the table by the door so the officer there can have a look in your bag, and at what's in your pockets, then you can go."

"Of course."

I picked up my bag off the floor and headed toward the door. A female and a male officer stood behind a table. Both wore gloves. Two ladies were ahead of me waiting for the female officer but the male officer had an empty table in front of him and beckoned Rafe over.

I surreptitiously watched as he emptied his pockets, curious as to what a modern vampire wouldn't leave home without. It wasn't much. His wallet and keys. That was it. The officer took a look through his wallet but there was nothing but credit cards, some cash and a few business cards.

He waited for me, presumably so we could walk back to the shop together.

When it was my turn, I gave my name and address to the officer and opened my bag for her. She took a flashlight and peered into my bag. In her other hand she wielded a black plastic stick for separating the items. As she poked around, my knitting needles pushed up out of my bag like skeletal arms.

Then she stopped moving and peered more closely into my bag.

I wished I hadn't brought my knitting. No doubt she was looking at all the dropped stitches.

I was about to explain that I was just a beginner, when she called, "Sir, can I see you over here?"

At her tone, Ian immediately came over. "What is it?"

He went behind the table, glanced at me curiously and then down into my bag. I wished I were neater and more tidy, like Rafe. There ought to be nothing in my bag but wallet, phone, maybe a lipstick. Not the piles of junk I was sure I'd need, the half packets of mints, old train tickets, used tissues, coins from every country I'd ever visited rattling around on the bottom.

There wasn't something witchy in there, was there? The thought had my heart stuttering. Ian's face went very still. He slipped on gloves and reached into my bag and pulled out a newspaper clipping.

"Would you like to explain?"

Sexy cop was gone, bad cop was back with a vengeance as he held up the folded newspaper clipping with Colonel Montague's photograph on it. The photograph had been defaced by a ball point pen crossed over the man's face.

If there was a correct response to a police officer showing you incriminating evidence he'd just taken out of your bag, I didn't know what it was. I think, for a good few seconds, we all stared at the clipping.

Then my frozen brain thawed. "That's not mine. I've never seen it before." My voice sounded high and shrill. I sounded exactly like Katie had when she'd tried to convince us all she was innocent. She must have felt this way, too, as though something hot and heavy was pressing on her lungs.

Ian slipped the newspaper clipping into an evidence bag.

"I'm telling the truth." I forced my voice to a lower register. "Someone must have put that into my bag."

I felt all eyes on me. The way everyone had stared at Colonel Montague in his final minutes, now they were focused on me. I felt so hot and flustered I wished I had something on under my sweater so I could pull it off.

"Let's finish this conversation down at the station."

I wanted nice Ian back. I glanced around as though he might be hiding somewhere, but all I saw were staring faces. "Are you arresting me?"

"We'd like you to come down to the station and help us with our enquiries."

What had I been doing for the last couple of hours? I felt coolness on the back of my neck and knew Rafe had moved closer to me. I'd never been gladder of his presence. "Lucy's telling the truth," he said. "She opened her bag when we left her shop, to show me her knitting. That clipping wasn't in there." He looked around the room. "Anyone could have dropped it in her bag."

The same 'anyone' who'd poisoned the colonel.

WHEN I RETURNED HOME from the most eventful afternoon tea I'd ever attended, I badly wanted to see my grandmother. It was nearly six when I returned to the shop.

It had been so humiliating, being driven to the police station. There weren't too many locals remaining in the church hall, but enough that I knew gossip would spread. I was escorted by the same cop who'd checked my bag. She wasn't a chatty type. Or maybe they aren't allowed to be friendly with the poor saps in the back of the police cruiser. Thames Valley police headquarters was a non-descript complex in Kidlington, tucked away behind a big hedge.

After waiting for half an hour in an uncomfortable waiting room chair, I was taken to an interview room. Ian and Detective Sergeant Elizabeth Drei asked me more questions, but I couldn't tell them what I didn't know. I said the paper wasn't mine, I'd never seen the colonel before or that newspaper. I think it helped that they were able to trace the clipping to an article in the London Times dated several months before. I'd been in Boston at the time.

After that, Ian asked me if I'd left my bag anywhere, or if anyone had sat particularly close to me. I was so tired of remembering details of the day. A man had been murdered before my eyes. Frankly, compared to that? Someone sitting beside me didn't rate very high.

However, since whoever had the clipping had obviously needed to get rid of it before they were searched, I tried to remember. Rafe had walked with me, the Irish woman had joined us and we'd walked over from the tea shop, chatting. I told Ian that she'd flipped the dead man the bird as he went by and then turned her back. I'd sat beside Katie aka Katya but I was certain one of us would have noticed if she'd slipped anything in my bag.

"Oh," I said, suddenly remembering. "I went to a corner to make a phone call and left my bag for, maybe, five minutes." I hadn't watched the bag. Anyone in the church hall could have slipped the clipping into it.

Ian tapped his fingertips together, making a soft slapping sound. He stared at the wall as though the beige paint fascinated him.

The article was about a review by the Ministry of Defense aimed at modernizing the British forces. Colonel Montague had been quoted, at length, as a retired colonel with strong views on how cutting numbers of personnel and reducing budgets had decimated the once proud British army. Could such opinions really have led to his death?

"That article has to be connected to his murder," I said. "Could he have angered someone who supports military cuts so much they'd kill him?"

He shifted his gaze to mine and I could see he didn't think much of my hypothesis. "Possibly. But it's more likely he upset someone while he was in the army."

He pointed to the few biographical facts supplied in the article, which he'd obviously studied before interviewing me. Now, he read, "Colonel Montague served in Germany in the 1960s, and as a young Lieutenant in Ireland in the 1970s." He glanced at me and I scrambled to recall my modern history. "The troubles?" I guessed. "The IRA?"

He nodded. Tapped his fingers some more. Said to DS Drei, "Check into the colonel's career. I'm especially interested in his term in Ireland."

I looked at him. "You think the Irish woman who acted so hostile to his corpse might have held a grudge for that long?"

"There are many avenues of enquiry in our investigation." Which I took to mean, 'keep your nose out of this.' But my nose had been shoved into a murder and, thanks to that planted paper, me and my nose had been dragged in for questioning. I thought I was entitled to speculate.

"Thank you for your cooperation," he said. "If you'd like to wait out front, someone will drive you home."

Someone? I wanted it to be Ian. There'd been so much flirty eye contact when we'd first met, I'd been certain he was going to ask me out. Now, I thought his murder case was more exciting to him than I was. Understandable, but hardly flattering.

I was standing outside in front of the station door, feeling pouty, wondering if they'd forgotten me and I'd have to get the bus back to Harrington Street, when a beat up old Mini Cooper pulled up. That was Ian's car. Suddenly, I knew I was at least as interesting as Colonel Montague's corpse.

My day was finally looking up.

So was Ian's. Not only could he drive me home, but I'd found out something interesting about the recently-departed colonel.

CHAPTER 6

"I thought you were going to send me home with a constable," I complained, as I slipped into the passenger seat beside Ian. The small car felt intimate and smelled of him, a subtle scent that was a combination of mint and rosemary. Unusual and very attractive.

He put the car into gear and we slid toward the exit. "Have to be careful, mixing business and pleasure," he said, cutting me a glance that made it clear which side of that equation I landed on.

I felt flustered and girly and resisted the urge to play with my hair. I was never very good at the whole flirting thing, and since I didn't know what to say, I said nothing.

Maybe he'd expected me to lob back the flirtation birdie, but, naturally, I dropped it onto soggy ground. There was silence for a few moments and then I remembered that even if I wasn't very good at flirting, I could do an internet search with the best of them.

I'd already exhausted everything the internet had on Ian

months ago, but Colonel Montague had proved quite interesting. "I found a more recent article on Colonel Montague," I said, feeling quite proud of myself.

"And what did you find?" He sounded like he was humoring me rather than salivating over my information. Whatever.

"This is from an article in The Daily Express. From May. Here's the headline: "'Army chiefs FURIOUS as British soldiers hounded over Northern Ireland Troubles,'" I read. "And the word furious is in all caps."

"The Express is a bit like that," he explained.

My jaw dropped. "Aren't you excited that your guess is probably right?"

He shrugged.

I waited. I might not be an Oxford detective, but I wasn't stupid. Sure enough, after a silence of about thirty seconds, he said, "Well? Are you going to read the rest of the article?"

Ha!

"'Former army chiefs are enraged at the government's refusal to grant amnesty for British soldiers who, they say, are being hounded over Northern Ireland's TROUBLES.' And Troubles is capitalized."

"Well, it was a big deal at the time. Still is."

"'Former soldiers in their sixties and seventies are facing prosecution over the killings in the 1970s.' Colonel Montague is quoted as saying, 'It's ridiculous to try and prosecute soldiers for things that happened nearly forty years ago. The British government kept detailed records, but the IRA kept none. It's simply unfair to prosecute us now. It's time for an amnesty.'"

"That's interesting."

"There's more. It says, 'Colonel Montague was a platoon commander in Belfast. He was involved in an incident in which an unarmed protestor was killed and several others badly wounded, including a priest who tried to intervene.'" I'd been thinking. If the Irish woman was seventy, she'd have been in her early twenties. "Could the Irish woman have had a brother, or lover, who was killed or injured? Maybe she held Colonel Montague responsible."

"But why wait so long to go after him?"

I flipped my hair over my shoulder. "I'm only the researcher, here. You're the detective."

He laughed at that. Then asked me how I was getting on with running the yarn shop. I told him I was enjoying it more than I'd imagined, though I steered clear of explaining about Gran and the vampires, obviously. Also, me being a witch was not a subject I wanted to talk about.

I longed for the days when my biggest problem around guys was being shy.

I WAS EXPECTING Gran and the rest of her undead friends at the knitting club that evening, but I didn't think I could wait that long to tell her what had happened.

"She'll be pleased to know you cast a successful spell today," Rafe said, having waited in the shop for my return.

"Pardon?" I'd had no thought of anything but the murder, but when I recollected the way I'd saved that tray from disaster, I realized he was right. Then I put my hands over my eyes and groaned. "What if that tray I saved from falling had the poisoned food on it? I may have helped the murderer!"

Rafe gave my horrible theory some thought and then said it was unlikely.

"I was supposed to practice with the grimoire this week but I've been so busy I haven't had much time." That was untrue. I was mostly just scared of the spell book.

"Knowing your grandmother she'll be so caught up in the excitement and gossip that she'll let you off lightly for not having completed your homework."

"I hope you're right." I'd planned to practice this evening before the knitting club. But, of course, I couldn't concentrate on casting spells or anything else until I had chatted over the murder in the tea shop with Gran.

He pushed away the carpet and opened the trap door in the back room. I went down the sturdy steps into the cavernous tunnels that crisscross underneath Oxford. We knocked in the correct pattern on the very undistinguished and barely visible ancient wooden door set into the stone. After observing us through the high-tech security system that Rafe had installed, Sylvia open the door.

Sylvia was one of the most elegant women I'd ever seen, alive or dead. She was a stage and film star in the 1920s. Not a household name, but she'd been successful. She had an air of glamor about her and always dressed beautifully. She'd been in her sixties when she was turned and her hair was a gorgeous silver that suited her large, gray-green eyes. Her figure was still stunning and she wore designer clothes that flattered her.

Considering she couldn't see her reflection, I was always impressed at how well she managed to turn herself out.

"Why, Lucy," she said. "What a surprise. We didn't expect

to see you until this evening." She glanced at my companion and said, "And Rafe. Always a pleasure."

"I didn't plan to come, but something extraordinary happened today and I have to talk to Gran."

Her finely pencilled brows rose in surprise, but she was either too well bred to pry or knew that I wouldn't say anything until my grandmother was in the room. "I know she's awake, I heard her moving around. Why don't you have a seat in the living room? I'll see if she's ready for company."

I'd have argued, since I've never had to use company manners with my grandmother, but now that Gran was a vampire, she had different routines. I thanked Sylvia and went to sit on one of the luxurious velvet settees.

Two vampires were sitting there, knitting, clearly trying to finish projects in time for tonight's show and tell. One was Silence Buggins who was the least silent person I'd ever known. She'd been born and lived in Victorian times and no matter that fashions and attitudes had changed, she still wore corsets, never exposed her ankles, and pinned her hair up on her head before ever leaving her home. In most places she'd have seemed very eccentric, but Oxford is full of oddly dressed people so she rarely got a second look.

While her needles moved so quickly her work was a blur, her lips moved almost as fast. "And so I said to him, if you mean to suggest that I am not fully conversant with the ways of the road, you are mistaken, sir. My bicycle most certainly had the right of way."

Alfred nodded and made sympathetic noises, but I don't think he was listening to her. I was deprived of the end of her harrowing tale, however. At a glance from Rafe, they both mumbled excuses, stowed their knitting into their bags, and left the room.

"You didn't need to throw them out," I said, shocked as always at the power he wielded.

"Terrible gossips, the pair of them. You can speak more openly without their noses in your business."

It was quite true, but he might have saved himself the trouble as my grandmother was a bit of a chatterbox herself.

I always felt mildly uncomfortable down here in their nest. The place was gorgeous, with antiques and art that had to be priceless. I suspected Sylvia had influenced the decorating. With the red velvet couches, the gilt and general air of opulence, it felt a bit like the setting for a silent movie. Still, being surrounded by so many vampires, especially in the early evening when they were just waking, made me a little nervous. Rafe, as though sensing my unease, said, "Can I get you something? A cup of tea?"

I shuddered. "I'm not sure I'll ever drink tea again."

"That's understandable but we don't know it was the tea that killed him. Depending on the poison and how quick-acting it is, the fatal dose could have been in the food he ate at the restaurant, something he ingested earlier in the day or even his medication."

"You mean it could've been an accident?"

He shook his head. "I doubt it. No, I believe he was murdered."

"How terrible for the poor Miss Watts."

He settled himself across from me, deliberating before he spoke. "I'm not sure about that."

He didn't elaborate and I found myself saying, "But they could lose the tea shop over this."

"They wouldn't be the first people who ever deliberately destroyed their business so they could claim the insurance money."

"You can't be serious. Are you suggesting that those lovely old ladies might have killed a man in order to get money?"

He shrugged. "I'm suggesting that rather than assuming the Miss Watts are also victims, we do a little research. Check into their finances. Do they have a written agreement of what happens if one of them wants out of the shop?"

I had so little to do with murder in my life, apart from my own grandmother's, of course, that it was almost inconceivable to me that one or both of those nice old ladies might have done something so despicable, but of course, there was evil in the world and only someone as naïve as I had once been would believe there wasn't. And they had been open to selling to that horrible developer who wanted to buy up our whole block. Also, with a new man causing trouble between them, maybe they'd be happy to split the insurance money and go their separate ways. "Don't most people who want to claim insurance burn down their businesses?"

"Arson's a tried and true method, certainly, but it's not the only one."

I wanted to argue further but I supposed he was right. Better to prove they were innocent and then we could move on to other more likely suspects. Like whoever put the incriminating newspaper clipping into my bag. At least they'd taken the Irish woman's name and had a copy of her ID. She shouldn't be difficult to find.

At that moment my grandmother came into the room. Her white hair was coiled into a bun as usual. Her kindly, placid face filled me with the same pleasure her appearance always did. She wore black trousers with a black diaphanous cloak that I think was crocheted. I'd come a long way in even being able to tell the difference between knitting and crochet. Vampire or not, Agnes Bartlett was still my grandmother. Moreover, she was someone who knew this neighborhood and most of the people who lived here.

"Lucy, I'm so pleased to see you. Will you have a cup of tea?"

Once more, I repressed the shudder the word tea caused to go down my spine. "No, thank you. I had some next door." And luckily Katya-AKA-Katie had managed to bring our correct order: One English Breakfast tea. Hold the poison.

Gran settled herself beside me and took my hand between her chilly ones. She looked into my face and I saw concern in her faded blue eyes. "But whatever's happened? You look as though you've had a shock."

"Oh I have." And then I told my grandmother everything that had happened that afternoon from the moment Rafe and I walked into the tea shop to the moment we left. Apart from a few interjections such as, "Oh my poor dear." And "Colonel Montague you say?" And "Whatever must Mary and Florence be going through?" She listened intently. Until she got to the part where the newspaper clipping was found in my bag. Then her hands flew to her mouth. "Oh, Lucy, how terrible for you. But who would do such a thing?"

CHAPTER 7

*R*afe didn't add anything to my recounting but he listened to every word carefully, almost as though he hadn't been there and were trying to see the events through my eyes. Sylvia sat quietly beside him. She also said nothing, though I could feel the intensity of her gaze.

After I had told Gran about the murder and my trip to the police station, I felt somewhat better. My throat was dry. I asked for some water. Sylvia fetched me a bottle and I drank thirstily.

Gran had been sitting, thinking. She said, "Colonel Montague, poisoned in the tea shop. It sounds like one of those children's board games, doesn't it?"

"Did you know him?"

She brought her focus back to me. "Oh yes. Yes. I knew him. Both Edward Montague and his wife, Elspeth. She used to knit, but she gave it up, said it hurt her eyes. I don't think that was the truth. I think he resented her spending the money."

I thought back to the man I had seen. He'd been wearing a good tweed jacket, gray woolen trousers and loafers. "He gave the air of being quite affluent."

"Oh, he's very rich, but tight as a tick. Poor Elspeth has always had a struggle to get any money out of him. If she had more gumption I'd suspect her of poisoning him herself."

Sylvia said, "Do you think she did? She was sitting across from him, so could easily have slipped poison into his tea. And she's likely the one who gains the most from his death."

Gran said, "They have two children. He was miserly and harsh with them, too. He was a thoroughly unlovable man."

Rafe said, "Any idea who his solicitor would be?"

"Yes. He used the same firm I did. Elliot, Tate and Mills. I know, because it was the colonel who recommended them to me. He might have been a dreadful man, but he was very astute about business."

Rafe stretched out his long legs in front of him. "I think I'll pay an after hours visit to the offices. Have a look at his will and see who benefits most from the man's death."

I felt this line of enquiry was preposterous. Children and wives didn't kill their husbands and fathers for money. And nice Irish ladies didn't go for tea with murder on their minds. And yet, of course, they did.

Sylvia said, "They say poison is a woman's crime." She smiled in reminiscence. "I played a woman like that once. In a play. She used rat poison to do away with her husband." She tilted her head as though accepting a bouquet of flowers. "I was very well reviewed."

"Was the woman in your play caught?"

"Yes. She was hanged for murder." She sighed and looked wistful. "My final scene brought down the house."

Rafe said, "Lucy suggested Colonel Montague might not even have been the intended victim. That waitress was hopeless and kept mixing up orders. She might have brought the poison to the wrong table."

Gran nodded. "But that assumes the poison was added to his food or drink in the kitchen. It seems to me that any number of people walking past a table in a busy restaurant could easily slip something into a man's tea, or his food. I don't suppose we know what sort of poison it was?"

It was Rafe who answered. "No. Could have been Cyanide or Strychnine, something that acts quickly. We won't know that until the post-mortem is completed."

Normally, of course, the police wouldn't share those results with a layperson but Rafe had the most incredible network of friends, informers, and the kind of creatures who can sneak in and out of locked buildings late at night without leaving a trace. I had no doubt we would have the results of the autopsy as soon as they were completed. Possibly before the police themselves.

"Who else was there?"

"I wish you'd been there, Gran. You'd have known everyone. There were some tourists, but lots of locals. Let me think. Bessie Yang, the yoga teacher was having tea with a doctor in her forties who attended to Colonel Montague when he became ill. Amanda Silvester.

"The Irish woman who had tea by herself and acted so strangely when the colonel's body went by. I'm convinced it was she who put the article in my bag.

"Miss Watt and Gerald Pettigrew were there, of course." I was ashamed that I'd only been in the tea shop myself in order to snoop on how the romance was going.

Gran shook her head. "Her behavior was shocking. She obviously hadn't warned Mary that she'd be a customer this afternoon. The sisters need to stick together in this terrible time."

"Maybe they will, but before the colonel died, there was definitely a fight brewing."

"What a shame that Gerald Pettigrew has caused friction between the sisters." She looked off into the distance. "Though I suppose it was to be expected."

"Do you remember him, Gran?"

"Oh, yes. Back then he was very good-looking and so charming. Neither of the Watt girls were ever much to look at, and I don't remember either of them having much of a social life. Then Gerald came along.

"Florence was like a woman transformed for the few months she and Gerald were together. I never found out what happened. Both sisters were very tight-lipped about the whole affair, but I do know that they didn't speak to each other for years after he left. If one came into the room the other would leave it. But, eventually, they buried the hatchet."

"I think the hatchet is back." I wondered if it would cleave them apart again.

Sylvia had said that poison was a woman's weapon and, while it's one of those old clichés of murder mysteries that I don't actually believe, I wondered. "Could the poison have been intended for Miss Watt's boyfriend? If Mary Watt really wanted to get rid of him..." I couldn't finish the thought. I flapped my hands in front of my mouth as though I could wave the words away. "Don't listen to me. It's a crazy idea."

"It's a perfectly valid theory, my dear. They all are at this stage. When we know so little. This murder is a puzzle with very few pieces and far too many blanks. But, if Mary Watt had set out to poison Gerald, I hardly think she would have left the delivery to an incompetent waitress. She's a very capable woman. If she'd intended him to die, the man would be dead."

It was rather a grim analysis of one of her dearest friends, but had a ring of truth to it. Mary Watt was certainly an efficient woman.

Rafe reminded us that Florence Watt and Gerald Pettigrew had swapped teapots and it was as likely that Florence was the intended victim. At that point my brain gave out. My thoughts were like a piece of my own knitting—a tangle of false starts and inexplicable knots making a shape that bore no resemblance to anything.

I went on trying to remember who was there. I said, "Oh, the table of ladies. One of them was called Miss Everly. She had three friends with her. They all went to St. Hilda's College and they were here for the funeral of a mutual friend. One of them was the verger for St. John's and she let us into the church hall."

Gran smoothed her skirt. "Sarah Everly?"

"I don't think we got her fist name," I said.

"It was Sarah," Rafe said. "I overheard the widow call her Sarah." Of course, his hearing was particularly acute.

"My goodness. Sarah Everly was once engaged to the colonel. That would have been in the late 1950s or the early 1960s, I imagine. They were both very young. She'd finished her degree and he was back from military college. Sandhurst, I believe."

"What happened?" She'd been introduced as Miss Everly,

so presumably if she hadn't married the colonel, she hadn't married anyone.

"He jilted her. For his current wife."

I recalled the attractive, blonde woman who had seemed a much more lively woman than the mousy colonel's wife. "But why?"

"Because Elspeth had a great deal of money. Oh, yes, it was a marriage based entirely on greed on his side and, poor soul, I believe genuine affection on hers."

"And Miss Everly never married?"

"No. She never did. She was better off without him, of course, but perhaps she didn't see being jilted as very good fortune."

The four women had seemed jolly and almost girlish discussing their old college days over glasses of sherry. "What did she study at school, do you know?"

"Biochemistry I believe."

We all stared at Gran and no one bothered to voice the obvious thought we all shared. A woman who had studied biochemistry would certainly know how to poison a man.

CHAPTER 8

*G*ran had been too preoccupied with all the news of the murder to question me about my progress with magic, but I knew my reprieve wouldn't last. I fully intended that by the time we met for the vampire knitting club that evening I would have something to report.

I thought I might as well use my powers, such as they were, for good and see if I could help solve the murder.

Katie and her boyfriend were the clear front-runners as suspects, given that they'd lied about so much. Had they killed the colonel?

But why? I couldn't focus on a spell, but I thought I might give the scrying mirror a try. It seemed to operate simply enough. I could ask to be shown a location, or what someone was doing, and the mirror would offer up that information. I think witches invented it so they could keep track of each other, before social media came along.

I tried to empty my mind, which was virtually impossible. I suspected that my abilities as a witch were on a par with

Katie's as a waitress. Not a comforting thought. I tried to put it aside, along with all the others that were crowding into my brain.

I looked at the mirror. It was so old the surface looked more like pewter than mirror. However, it was a beautiful piece, with a heavy gold frame studded with symbols and jewels that might actually be real. It had never been stolen, which made me believe there was a powerful spell on it.

Gran had taught me to focus on one question. I recited the brief incantation that opened the magic, rather the way a password might open a computer file, and the surface began to ripple. I was in. Allowing myself a moment to enjoy the euphoria of having completed step one in using the scrying mirror, I asked the question that was obsessing me.

"Show me Jim and Katie in their flat." I had no idea what their last name was or where this flat might be located and I was sure there were plenty of Jims and Katies in the world.

But, it turned out that scrying mirrors had much more powerful magic than computer search engines. I began to see a shape, almost like a very old photograph faded by light and time so that the outlines were only barely visible. As I watched, focusing and repeating the question in my mind, the picture became clearer and sharper. And soon I recognized the very Katie and Jim that I wanted. Katie was in Jim's arms and she was crying.

He had his arms wrapped around her and, I could see what Katie could not, helpless bafflement on his face. He patted her back awkwardly. There was no audio, only visual, but I imagined he was saying the kind of pointless platitudes a man says to a crying woman. "There, there. Don't cry. Everything's going to be okay." And so on.

His words had the same effect that most men's have on crying women. None at all. She continued to cry and he continued to pat her back awkwardly.

The flat itself looked nondescript and uninteresting. It was like student digs anywhere. There was an old kitchen with a pile of dishes on the counter that needed washing, and behind that a sitting room with shabby furniture that probably came with the rental. The window was shuttered so I couldn't see what was outside. In fact, although I could see what they were doing, I had no idea where they were. I watched them for a few more minutes until I began to feel like a voyeur and then the image faded back to mirror.

Still, I was mildly triumphant. This was the second time I had got the scrying mirror to work. The first time, I believed, was beginner's luck but this time I'd definitely done it properly.

I glanced at my watch and saw that I had less than thirty minutes before the vampire knitting club started. I tidied my hair, changed into a fresh pair of jeans and put on one of the sweaters my grandmother had knitted me. Then I went downstairs.

There were normally about ten or twelve vampires who came to the biweekly knitting circle but instinct told me that now there'd been a murder we'd have a larger crowd.

I had learned a few things about vampires in the time I'd known the knitting group. I appreciated that they used to be terrifying creatures of the night who would pounce on anyone unwitting enough to stray alone down a dark alley at night, particularly sweet young virgins, but times had changed. Of course, there were still rogue vampires who killed for the sport, but most of them found it much easier and more convenient to use blood banks. Certainly the private blood bank run by Doctor Weaver kept the local vamps well supplied. The biggest problem for vampires was not getting their next meal, but was boredom. So, I knew perfectly well, that given the challenge of helping solve a murder, a larger number of our local group than usual would be in my knitting shop this evening.

I set up twenty chairs in a large ragged circle. It was quiet with only the sound of the chairs scraping on the wooden floor as I arranged them. Nyx sat in the corner of the room keeping a managerial eye on things and licking her paws to pass the time.

Even without her suddenly widening her eyes and looking past me, I knew I wasn't alone from the cold prickling on the back of my neck. I turned, and there was Rafe. "I thought you might need help setting up. I should warn you there will be a larger than usual turnout tonight."

Then he saw the number of chairs I had laid out. "You worked that out for yourself."

He began to neaten the chairs into a more perfect circle while I went into the front and made sure the blinds were fully closed so as to prevent anyone on the outside from seeing lights on in the shop.

Gran and Sylvia arrived first as they usually did. I was so excited by my adventures with the scrying mirror that I rushed up to my grandmother and told her of my success.

"That's wonderful, dear. I was hoping you hadn't let your training lapse."

"No, of course not. I worked with the scrying mirror and I was able to see Jim and Katie in their flat."

"That's very promising. What were they doing?" I wasn't

sure if she was asking me to gauge my magic powers or because she wondered what the two possible murderers had been doing when no one was watching. I suspected the latter.

"They had their arms around each other and Katie was crying," I reported.

Gran said how proud she was of me. "But I do wish we knew more. Whoever murdered the colonel may strike again. In fact, I've been thinking, the funeral those women from St. Hilda's attended, do we know how their friend died?"

I hadn't thought to connect the death of an old college friend with that of Colonel Montague, but Rafe had. He said, "I checked. The friend died of natural causes. She was in her eighties and suffered a massive heart attack. With her obesity and her smoking habit I'm surprised she lasted that long."

"Well that is a relief. So we're only looking at one murder, not a serial killer."

I could've sworn my grandmother sounded disappointed at only having a single murder to solve. But I was tired, perhaps I was imagining things.

There was a low rap on the front door and I jumped. I'd just finished making sure not a chink of light could show from the street. Who could be knocking on the door? Rafe said, "I'll get that."

"Ignore it. They'll go away," I said.

"I don't want them to go away. I asked this person to stop by."

We all watched him tread slowly toward the front door. In truth, it was no hardship watching Rafe walk. The only other person I've ever seen with that walk is Colin Firth. It's long-limbed. He leads with his hips and swings his shoulders in a very attractive fashion. From the way the other women were watching him, I did not think I was the only person who thought so.

He peered briefly between the slats of the blinds and then unlocked the door and opened it. In walked a man I had seen him briefly greet outside the tea shop. They'd spoken briefly, and then the man had continued on his way while the rest of us were herded to the church hall.

Rafe brought him all the way through to the back room and he glanced around with interest. He nodded to all of us in a very courtly way. "Good evening, ladies."

Rafe said, "This is a friend of mine. Anthony Billing. Did you find anything?"

"Oh yes. It was easy enough to follow them." He had a very pleasant Scottish burr. "After the police officer took the pair to the station, I had a wee snoop."

"And what did you find?" My grandmother asked eagerly.

"Well, dear lady, they are exactly who they say they are. Their names are Katherine Ainsley and James Walker. They met in acting school in Melbourne. After they graduated, neither of them achieved much success. He was in a couple of commercials and has done a lot of community theatre, while she very nearly had a big break being cast in a pilot for a show that sadly was never picked up by a network. I get the feeling they thought they might have better opportunities here."

"And was he a chef?" I had to ask. I'd eaten his scones and they were certainly tasty.

"Oh yes, yes, indeed. In fact, it's my belief he should stick to cooking. I think it's a more viable career than this acting business."

"Could you find any connection at all to Colonel Montague?"

"No, I'm afraid not. There's one interesting thing though."

"What's that?"

"According to her diary, he wants to marry her as soon as they are on a better footing, financially. They're living hand to mouth, those two."

"Could someone have paid them to kill the colonel?" I asked. I was clutching at straws, I knew.

He appeared to consider my question seriously. "As hired assassins, you mean? Well, I suppose it's possible. It will depend on the will. And what happens to the colonel's estate, and whether this pair suddenly come into money."

I had no doubt at all that Rafe and his vampire network would keep tabs on Katie and Jim's bank accounts. Rafe and his friend had done better than I had with my scrying mirror.

"Do you knit, sir?" My grandmother asked him. "Our little knitting circle meets in a few moments and you'd be most welcome to join us."

"Oh thank you very much. But no, I've got papers to grade tonight."

"I quite understand," said my grandmother at her most gracious. "We meet every Tuesday and Thursday at ten o'clock at night. You'd always be welcome."

He thanked her and then walked back to the front door. I let him out and firmly locked and bolted the door behind him.

Papers to grade? "Is your friend a professor at one of the colleges?" I asked Rafe in a whisper.

"Oh, yes. You'd be amazed how many of the dons are undead."

CHAPTER 9

*W*e had so many people at the vampire knitting club that night that I needed more chairs. There were twenty-three of us altogether. We conducted our meeting on the usual lines, beginning with the show and tell, where everyone displayed the project they were currently working on and asked for any advice that was needed. Then, we all settled to work.

I worked on the pair of socks I had begun several weeks ago. I felt better at least attempting to fit in, but I sensed that we all rushed through the preliminaries in order to get to the best part of the evening's entertainment.

The gossip.

All the vampires wanted to help solve the murder, not out of altruism, but for something to do.

I said, "I think I need to go back to yoga." I patted my belly where indeed the flesh had grown a little slack of late. "I need to tighten my core. I'll go to a lesson with Bessie and then try and chat with her afterwards. Find out if she knows or saw anything."

My grandmother said, "Excellent. And we need to find a way to talk to Elspeth Montague, the colonel's widow. I can't do it because she will recognize me, and she's already had enough of a shock, losing her husband. She doesn't want to see an old friend come back from the dead."

We all agreed that would be somewhat disconcerting. Sylvia said, "She doesn't know me. I could pose as a florist, delivering flowers on her bereavement. You may safely leave it to me to talk my way into her confidence."

"What about the doctor?" I asked. "Is there any point learning more about her?"

Silence Buggins was desperate to be involved. The poor woman wanted nothing more than to be the center of attention, but her incessant chatter, instead of giving Silence her wish, caused people to walk away when she was speaking to them or tune her out. She said, "I could go to the doctor. I could pretend I was suffering the vapors, or, perhaps, consumption." She put her hand to her mouth and coughed in a most ladylike manner.

Sylvia and Gran exchanged a glance and both shook their heads infinitesimally. Sylvia said, "Silence, dear, consumption, now called tuberculosis, is very rare these days. And no one's gone to a doctor with 'the vapors' in more than a century. Besides, what do you think will happen when the doctor examines you?"

Silence looked so disappointed that Alfred paused in his knitting and said, "Perhaps you could try and sell her something."

"Like what?"

Hester, the eternal surly teenager, said, "Tickets to a fancy dress play, I should think. You look enough of a freak that she might believe that."

Silence would've grown red in the face had she had enough blood in her body to do so. As it was, she stiffened whatever part of her wasn't already stiffened by the whalebone in her corsets. "I will not be spoken to in such an insolent manner."

"Actually," I said, "That's not a bad idea. Tell her that one of the colleges is putting on a play about... about..." I looked around me, "Female doctors in Victorian times?"

"There were a few," Dr. Weaver said, nodding.

"She's a female doctor, she's bound to take an interest. You can get her talking about the terrible tragedy."

Silence brightened up immediately. "Yes. That's an excellent idea, Lucy. I'll do it."

Hester rolled her eyes and began stabbing her needles into her wool. My grandmother, always one to try and make people feel good about themselves, said, "That was an excellent suggestion, Hester. Perhaps you might befriend the young man. The chef, Jim."

"I'm sixteen years old. Don't be disgusting."

"I didn't mean like that. Tell him you've seen him working in the kitchen at the tea shop and that you're hoping to become a chef yourself one day."

"I suppose," she said in her usual bored tone, but I noticed she stopped stabbing the wool as though she were trying to murder it and actually began to knit. It was a start.

By the time we ended the meeting, everyone who wanted to take part in our investigation had a job and those who didn't had agreed to keep their ears and eyes open as they went around Oxford and report back any interesting tidbits of information. It was amazing what vampires, with their powerful hearing, overheard in pubs or on the street.

"What about you, Rafe?" I noticed he hadn't taken a task. He looked at me with one of his cool smiles. "I'm going to look into Colonel Montague's past. And, I think, into Gerald Pettigrew's."

"Do you think he could have killed the colonel or been the intended victim?"

"Either. But I like Florence and Mary Watt. If that man's got secrets, I intend to find them before he can cause any trouble."

"But Florence is so happy."

"And we want her to stay that way."

"What about you, Lucy?"

Before I could answer, Sylvia said, "Obviously, Lucy will be our liaison with DI Ian Chisholm, who cannot keep his eyes off her."

I felt myself growing hot. "That's not true."

"Of course it is. Use his infatuation to get information."

I felt Rafe's cool gaze on me and blushed more hotly. "I'm not, he's not—"

It was Alfred, the long-nosed vampire who rescued me. "Good heaven's, girl, whatever have you done to that sock? It looks like something you'd use to scrub the pots."

I glanced down and to my horror he was right.

"Try to untangle it with a spell," Gran said, trying to turn my knitting disaster into a teaching moment.

What I really wished for was a disappearing spell.

CHAPTER 10

The following day started out uneventful, at least in
Cardinal Woolsey's. Next door at Elderflower was
a different matter. Police vehicles arrived, and forensics teams
went in. Every once in a while, they'd leave with a box or a
bag, looking very official and very mysterious.

Agatha and I pretended it was business as usual, but both
of us spent more time than necessary at the front of the shop,
tidying and rearranging the window display, which gave us
an excellent view of the street.

While I was placing one of the hand-knit sweaters, along
with a pattern and the wools and needles to make it, into the
front window display, disturbing Nyx, who meowed at me in
annoyance, a television news crew showed up. The death had
been on the news last night, but I suppose they wanted fresh
footage for this evening's update.

I'd learned a bit about Colonel Montague, but nothing
that would explain why he was murdered in the Miss Watts'
tea shop. According to last night's news report, the colonel

had been born in 1945, was educated at Eton and Sandhurst. He'd served in Germany and then been stationed in Ireland during 'the troubles' in the 1970s. After that, he'd worked in administrative roles until he retired. The report mentioned that he left a wife and two children.

Perhaps if I hadn't been such a busybody, with so much of my attention on what was going on next door, I might have prevented the disaster that happened in my own shop.

There were no customers at the time.

I was staring out the front window when Nyx growled and looked behind me, her eyes as round as twin moons.

I turned and my grandmother was standing in the shop, looking around as though she didn't know where she was. She was more than half asleep and, before I could gather my wits, she said to Agatha, "Hello. Can I help you?"

Agatha stared at Gran and then pointed a trembling finger at the lovely framed memorial photograph of her, including the date of her death. "*Mon Dieu*," she croaked. "*Vous êtes mortes!*" Then she crossed herself. Still gabbling in French she dashed for the door.

Where a TV News crew was standing right outside.

Do something.

What? I looked at Gran but she was in some twilight world still.

I didn't have time to run upstairs and get the grimoire. There was no time to think, so I acted. I got between Agatha and the door. "Agatha, wait. There's a perfectly simple explanation."

She stared at me and back at Gran and made the sign of the cross once more. "*Non.* Get out of my way." She began to push past me.

Desperation lent sharpness to my memory. I managed to recall a page I'd read last night. A forgetting spell. I admit I was thinking of banishing all memories of Todd, aka The Toad, former boyfriend and betrayer. It was the last thing I'd read before I fell asleep.

I looked at Agatha, right into her startled, fearful eyes. We locked gazes and, as I felt her fear, I was filled with compassion for this poor woman who'd suffered such a shock. For her sake as well as ours, I drew all my concentration to the fore and banished doubts.

Nyx was a warm presence brushing against my legs and I drew energy from her as well.

In a low voice, I recited:

Forgetful of this time and place
Go on your way with peace and grace
This memory is nothing but dust
Blown away and the feelings lost

Here, I raised my hand, palm up and blew on it, picturing her recent memory wafting away.

As I will it, so mote it be

There was absolute silence. I held my breath. Agatha blinked and glanced around, looking confused, but no longer frightened. "*Qu'est-ce qui ce passé?*"

I fetched her handbag. "I'm so sorry we couldn't help you find the wool you wanted," I said, hoping I sounded professional. "Have a nice day."

I opened the door for her and she walked out, looking around her as though unsure where she was. The reporter, standing idle as they waited for more happenings next door, walked over to her, mic at the ready. "Do you work here?"

Agatha glanced at him and then back to where I had the

door already half closed. She had the look of someone arriving in an airport after a very long flight. "No. I've never been here before." And then she walked away.

I found the 'back in ten minutes' sign and put it on the door. Then I turned to Gran, trying to keep the frustration out of my voice. "Gran! What are you doing here?"

Gran looked as confused as Agatha. And sleepy. "I don't know. I woke up and realized I was late to open the shop." She spotted the photograph and walked over to study it. "Oh, that's a nice photo of me. Usually, I look such a frump in photos. I'm very uncomfortable in front of the camera." She read the dates of her birth and death and then put a hand over her mouth. "Oh, I remember now. I'm not supposed to be here, am I? It's so difficult to remember I'm dead."

"I know." How could I stay mad when she looked so guilty?

"And I frightened that poor woman. Was she your new assistant?"

I shrugged. "She wasn't very good, anyway. Very superior."

"You did a nice job with that forgetting spell. Fudged the rhyme a little, but not so anyone would notice." As though I'd played a wrong note at my piano class recital.

"Don't the words have to be exact?"

"Not really. The rhyme helps you focus. Once you get practicing, my dear, you'll be a very powerful witch."

"Powerful enough to stop you coming into the shop at all hours?"

Her eyes twinkled when she looked at me. "Probably not. I was a witch long before you were born."

And having put me in my place, she walked into the back

room and I heard her open and close the trap door that would lead her back to her bed.

I was going to have to get cracking with my spell book. Either I was going to go through a lot of assistants, or I was going to find a powerful spell to keep that trap door closed. More powerful than Gran's ability to break it.

I'd never imagined having a power struggle with my own grandmother.

Certainly not a magic one.

With no assistant, I didn't get a lunch break. Since I didn't have a half-crazed Frenchwoman telling people my dead grandmother was walking around the shop in the middle of the day, either, I decided it was a reasonable trade-off.

I placed an advertisement in my window saying I was looking for an assistant. It didn't take long. I just put up the same notice I'd used a week ago.

At the end of the day, I went to the bank with a disappointingly small deposit and then popped into the grocer's where I put another notice on the community board for a shop assistant.

The woman who ran the grocer's regarded me over the top of her glasses. "What? Another assistant?" She looked at me as though perhaps I beat my employees or locked them in the basement between shifts.

I smiled, in what I hoped was a carefree manner. "It's so hard to find good help these days."

"Not if you pay them well and treat them right." She was so smug. The only person she employed was her henpecked husband. He was hard of hearing, which was probably why they were still married.

After I pinned up my notice he wandered out of the stock

room, carrying a box of breakfast bars. He began unloading them onto the shelf with the cakes and cookies. She saw him and shrieked. "No, Dennis. I said Digestive biscuits, not Weetabix! Go back and do it again, you silly fool."

"Thank you for the excellent labor relations advice," I said, as I left.

She wasn't the only one who could do smug.

CHAPTER 11

The next day, I put a spell on the trap door to protect me from evil coming in. It was all I could find in my grimoire, when what I really wanted was a spell to prevent embarrassment, in the form of my grandmother turning up in the shop.

If I were writing a spell book, I'd put anti-embarrassment spells at the top of the list.

It was another quiet day and there was no sign of activity next door at Elderflower. Maybe working on my knitting might help calm me. I don't know why I thought that. It was what knitters said. To me, knitting was an ordeal, me versus a squishy ball of animal hair, and, of course, the squishy animal hair always triumphed.

Even though the sock pattern was meant to be easy, level-one-beginner, easy, I did not find it so. We all have different talents and I am sad to say that knitting was not one of mine.

Normally this wouldn't matter very much but since I had

unfortunately inherited a knitting shop. I should at least learn how to knit a pair of socks.

When the door opened and the bell jingled, announcing a new customer. I was happy to put down my needles. This sock would only fit a pig or cow or something with a very tiny foot and a very long, skinny calf. I'd have to unpick it and start again.

I glanced up and was shocked to see Katie, formerly-known-as-Katya walk in. She looked a bit sheepish and blushed when she saw my obvious surprise. However, a shop is a public place. I couldn't throw her out, so I asked, cool and professional, "Hello. Can I help you?"

She looked ill-at-ease and gave the impression that she'd rather be a thousand miles away. That would have suited me, too. She said, "I see you're looking for a shop assistant."

There was a pause. Was she seriously suggesting herself as a candidate? This girl who couldn't carry a tray without dropping it, couldn't bring a pot of tea without getting the wrong table, and had pretended to be someone entirely different than she was. Oh, yes, and she was a suspect in a murder.

She could probably see those thoughts running across my face, and said quickly, before I could tell her she wasn't suitable, "I'm a very good knitter."

"Really?" It was all I could come up with.

She pulled her mouth to one side as though she'd eaten something sour. "Much better than I am a waitress."

Well, if she wanted to prove she could knit, I had the perfect project. I pushed the tangle of pig socks onto the counter. "If you can fix this mess and turn it into a pair of socks, suitable for a human, you're hired."

I admit, I hadn't really thought this through. Because, even if she was as good a knitter as my grandmother, she was a terrible choice as my shop assistant. First, I didn't trust her. Second, she was nothing like the assistant I wanted. In my mind, my ideal employee was someone very much like my grandmother, an older woman who was an excellent knitter and understood patterns as well as having some sales ability. Katie appeared to have none of these things.

However, she picked up the tangled mess and studied it. "What happened? Did the cat get hold of this?"

"No," I said. "It was me. The truth is I can't knit to save my life, and, since I run a knitting shop, I felt like I should learn. But it's not going very well."

She didn't run back into the street. And she didn't laugh at me. She laid the mess out flat and studied it critically. "Your first problem is that you're pulling your wool too tight."

I began to get an inkling that this woman who lied about everything might actually know something about knitting.

She glanced at me uncertainly. "Do you mind if I unpick this and start again?"

I thought of all the hours and swearwords that had gone into the current mess. But, it was never going to be a pair of socks so we might as well reuse the wool. "Sure."

Very efficiently she unravelled the mess and pulled my stitches out. The wool snagged a few times and she had to stop and unknot some gnarly bits, but I could tell from the way her fingers moved that she had an affinity with wool. People are given different gifts. Some people can sit down at a piano keyboard and feel the music, others can paint or write or understand math, or waitressing.

Katie had no talent for waitressing, but I began to think she might be good with the needles.

When she finished rewinding the wool into a ball, she settled herself in my visitor's chair, picked up the pattern and studied it briefly and then she began to knit.

My fingers were actually aching from the effort I had put into the several rows I'd mangled today, but there was a fluidity to the way her fingers moved. It was rhythmic and soothing.

"Well, if you want to sit here and knit, I suppose I should interview you." In this I was being somewhat sneaky. I didn't plan to hire her; I was doing some amateur sleuthing. Interviewing the suspect.

"Great." She was more relaxed now she was knitting. I wanted her at her ease.

"Tell me about yourself?" Such a wonderful open question that everyone hates on a job interview.

She did a few more stitches and said, "I was born in Melbourne but we moved to Sydney when I was child. I learned to knit from my grandmother. She looked after me when Mum was at work." She glanced up at me and back at her work and she sounded like a much softer Katie than the one who'd been working next door. "It makes me feel close to her when I knit."

"I feel that way about my grandmother, too. Being in this shop, I mean. Obviously. she failed at teaching me to knit."

Katie smiled at that. "I was gutted when my granny died. But she was old and it was her time. I never really got over losing her. Anyway, after I finished school, I worked in a knitting and craft store in Melbourne. I could give you the email address of the owner. In fact, I'd be working there, still, if Jim hadn't talked me into this trip."

I was leaning my back against the cash desk. The way the knitting was flowing for her, made her words easier. "Tell me about you and Jim."

She stopped, checked the knitting pattern and then went back to her work. "Not much to tell," she said. "We met at Melbourne Academy of Dramatic Arts. MADA, though of course, we shortened it to MAD. I was never cut out for uni and I don't think Jim was either. We both loved acting and wound up in the same improv class."

"Improv? I can't imagine."

"It was good fun. He's always been a joker and a good mimic. He'd pull stunts all the time pretending to be other people. He said it was good practice. When we finished the course, we got work here and there, but not enough to live on. He made his living as a cook and I worked in the knitting shop. When he suggested we should chuck it all and move to England for a year, I thought he was joking."

"But he wasn't."

She had the toe piece already finished and it looked like human toes would be quite comfy in there. I was impressed. "Australians love to travel. It's in our nature. Jim really wanted to get away. He said that while we're young and don't have children that's when we should be traveling. I suppose he's right."

"And you chose Oxford?"

"We spent a few days in London, but he wanted to come to Oxford. Said once we got home we could always tell 'we'd gone to Oxford.'" She rolled her eyes at Jim's foolishness. "Like I said, he's a joker."

Her fingers moved so quickly and surely it was a pleasure to watch them. "Well, when we got here, we had a bit of a holiday. One day, we walked up this street and he said he wanted to take me for a proper English tea. But we had to pretend we were Polish. Just for a joke, you know."

"Why Polish?"

"No reason. The day before we'd pretended to be Italians for the day."

"So, you went into Elderflower as pretend Poles."

"Yes. It was Miss Mary Watt who sat us. Then her sister came in with her fellow. And there was clearly something going on. Florence said they were going out, miffy like. Mary said, "Who do you think is to do all the cooking? And take care of the customers?"

"They argued like that in front of their guests?"

"Oh, yes. You can imagine how the rest of the argument went, and then Florence went off with her man. Jim said that was our chance. We finished our tea and dashed back to the flat. He got me to take off all my makeup and dress in a simple skirt and a new top with a high neck and long sleeves. And he put on his best jeans and his nice shirt. He said we'd tell Miss Watt we were brother and sister and had to work together. I thought it was mad, but we went round there and the poor old lady was in a state. A large party of Germans arrived in front of us. She nearly wept."

"Oh, poor Miss Watt." I couldn't believe how thoughtless Florence had turned out to be when blinded by infatuation.

"I don't think she would ever have hired us if she wasn't desperate. And, Jim being Jim, of course, he made her a deal. He said that if we didn't get her through that day without any complaints she could fire us on the spot.

Wouldn't owe us a penny. She was that desperate that she said yes."

"So that's how you never had to show her identification or provide any references."

"That's right. After the first day, when Jim turned out all the scones and the sandwiches and the quiches better than they can do themselves, she said she'd keep us on. He's quick, you see. A lovely cook."

"Bold, too."

"I don't think she liked me, not right from the first, but Jim said we were a pair and so I s'pose she decided to lump it. She probably thought she could train me. But it was awful work. I'd never be a waitress. Never again."

Probably a blessing to every food establishment on the planet.

"It was fun at first, pretending to be Polish. Like being on stage all the time. The only time we spoke normally was in our flat. He insisted, even when we were on the street, we had to stay in character."

"Well, I'm not as trusting as Miss Watt. I would like the name and email address and phone numbers of the craft shop where you worked. "

She glanced up, looking pleased. "You mean you'll hire me?"

When she'd come in, I'd had no intention of doing so. But the way that woman knit was like watching someone sit down at the piano expecting chopsticks and they came out with a Beethoven concerto. Her knitting was poetry in motion. Already a sock was emerging.

"I assume you've got some kind of a work visa?"

She nodded.

She gave me her mobile number and the information I'd asked for and I said I'd be in touch.

She looked sorry to part from the partial sock. "Would you mind if I took this home with me? I haven't had a knitting project in such a long time and it calms me down. It's a bit stressful right now, as you can imagine."

"Was it awful, with the police?"

She shuddered. "It wasn't pleasant. If we hadn't pretended to be Polish it would have been better. I'd never have agreed to be Katya if I'd imagined she'd see someone die."

As bad as it had been for me, sitting in Elderflower Tea Shop as a customer, I could see it had been worse for her, the person who had presumably carried the poison that killed Colonel Montague.

"Yes," I said. "Of course you can take the socks home."

I suppose I was taking a chance that I might never see wool, pattern, socks, or Katie ever again but I didn't think any of them would be a great loss.

She gathered up her things. "I hope you hire me. I don't even care what the pay is. I need something to do. I keep seeing him you see."

From the number of times I had relived that terrible scene in the tea shop I could only imagine what it was like for her. "Is there anything you can remember, anything you saw, that you maybe forgot to tell the police?"

"I've racked my brains, really I have, the only thing I can think of is the rat poison."

CHAPTER 12

A shudder quite as dramatic as hers went over my whole body. "Rat poison?"

"I wasn't to tell anyone. It's a terrible deep, dark secret, but Jim saw a rat when he was tidying up the supplies."

"A rat?" I know I shrieked like a girl, but I am a girl, and besides, the tea shop was only next door. I could only imagine how cozy rats might find a nice basket of wool to curl up into. And they could pop next door for the smorgasbord of food. What self-respecting rat wouldn't want to live in our neighborhood?

I was so glad Nyx had adopted me.

"He said it was just a baby rat." As though that made it better. Where there were baby rats there must be parents and brothers and sisters, cousins and aunts, second cousins three times removed.

I'd just about got used to living with a nest of vampires, I didn't think I could take a nest of rats as well. I'm a tolerant woman but I can only go so far.

"Anyway, he told Miss Watt and, naturally, she had a fit. Next thing she came into the kitchen with rat poison and told him and me we mustn't tell a soul. Jim said there are rats in every kitchen but Miss Watt claimed there'd never been one in hers.

If there was rat poison in the kitchen, it would be easy to slip some to a customer.

Who had access to the kitchen? Both Miss Watts obviously Jim and Katie, and who else? I didn't know, so I asked Katie the question.

She wrinkled her brow. "Day before yesterday, you mean?"

"Yes, I suppose so."

"Well, all the people you said, of course. And Mr. Pettigrew. Florence Watt's gentleman friend. He came in to ask about the quiche recipe. I didn't really listen. One of the old ladies came in mistaking the kitchen for the toilet. That happens at least once a day. It's not signed properly and people walk right into the kitchen instead of going up the stairs."

"Old lady? What old lady?"

"I don't know their names. There was a table of four of them. I didn't serve them."

Miss Everly and her friends. "But if you saw that lady come in, presumably you turned her around and directed her to the washroom."

"Oh yes. But what if she came back when there was no one there?"

I felt my eyebrows draw together in a puzzled frown. "Why would there be no one there?"

She looked as though she wished she hadn't spoken.

104

"Look, I don't want to get him in trouble, but Jim smokes." She glanced up at me and then out the window. "In fact, we both do. We'd sneak outside for a smoke break when it wasn't too busy."

"I see. So there were times when there wasn't anyone in the kitchen. And every person in the restaurant had access to rat poison."

"I suppose so. Plus, someone could have come in the street door. The kitchen opens onto the back alley."

It seemed the police had their work cut out for them. And speaking of work, this was supposed to be a job interview. "So, you smoke."

"Only about three ciggies a day. One after breakfast, and then I have another one on my lunch hour, and another after dinner. Honestly, if I worked here, I wouldn't sneak out. You could trust me."

Nothing about her recent activities should fill me with trust but, oddly, I did trust her. Maybe I was a fool, but my instinct said that she was a good person at heart. Nyx, who'd been snoozing in the front window, where three tourists had taken her picture, suddenly stood and stretched. Then she stepped daintily out of the basket, hopped down, walked straight over to Katie and butted her nose against the Australian girl's leg.

She said, "Well, look at you." When she picked the cat up, Nyx curled into her arms, made a contented sound and then stared at me with her green eyes. Some people say cats aren't good communicators but I can only say they should meet Nyx.

I felt certain the cat was confirming my judgement that Katie was someone I could trust. She certainly let herself be stroked under the chin and cooed to. She rewarded Katie by purring loudly. I couldn't help but laugh. "Nyx likes you."

Katie was laughing too. When she smiled her whole face lit up. "Does her opinion count?"

I looked at Nyx. We hadn't been together long but she was already a very important part of my life. "Oh yes, Nyx's opinion definitely counts."

The minute Katie had left I got on my computer to search for the shop she'd worked in. Nyx jumped into the window and peered out the window, watching Katie walk away.

One of the nice things about having Nyx was being able to talk aloud to her without looking like a crazy person. "You liked her, didn't you?"

Nyx licked her front paw.

"You don't think we're running a risk hiring someone who's a possible suspect in a murder?"

Nyx yawned.

I wasn't precisely sure how far ahead Melbourne time was from Oxford time, but I thought the sooner I sent my email, the sooner I'd get a reply. I was impressed by their website and at the breadth of offerings. They offered the usual knitting and crochet, but they'd added spinning, weaving and felt-making. An upcoming class on dyeing your own wool looked interesting.

Having sent off my email asking questions about Katie's work history, attitude, punctuality and her honesty, I checked my incoming emails. There was one from my mother. I hoped she was setting a date to come back to England for visit, as she and my dad had been promising to do since I moved to Oxford.

However, they were incredibly busy at the archaeological

dig in Egypt. "Mummies can be so demanding," I said aloud, then giggled at my bad pun. She said the dig was going well and that they might come to Oxford to recruit some new students to work with them, but that probably wouldn't be for a few months.

There was also an email from my friend Jennifer, back in Boston. She was full of news about our friends back home and was already making plans for Christmas. A bunch of my old pals were renting an apartment in New York for New Year's. It sounded like so much fun.

I felt the pull of homesickness. I didn't have any friends my own age here. Mostly, because I'd been too busy to go out and socialize. And the invitations I had received, like the witch pot luck dinner, weren't exactly thrilling me. I spent most of my free time with a bunch of vampires who were centuries older than I was.

The bell jingled telling me I had customers so I closed my email and put away my momentary homesickness with it.

It was Saturday and I was fairly sure I'd be spending my Saturday night with Nyx and my spell book. I also knew I'd start going through my wardrobe trying to decide what to wear on my Sunday afternoon date with a vampire.

CHAPTER 13

Sunday was a dry day. Cloudy in the morning, but as the day advanced, the sun came out. I tried on pretty much everything in my closet before settling on my black skinny jeans, boots and the cranberry colored sweater pattered with falling leaves that Alfred had knit for me. I left my hair loose and put more than usual effort into my makeup, which is to say about five minutes instead of the usual two.

I was standing outside waiting when a sleek black car drew up soundlessly. Behind my sunglasses, I rolled my eyes. Of course he was driving a Tesla.

I got into the car and he pulled away. I realized I was excited and wondered how much of my pleasure was at getting away from the shop and the proximity to the murder scene next door.

"Nice car."

"Thank you."

"Very environmentally friendly."

He smiled at that. "I have more reason than most to worry about the future of the planet."

We drove out of the center of Oxford and into the leafy suburban streets with their brick Victorian homes, but he kept going and I realized we were heading out of town. "I have no idea where you live."

"Near Woodstock."

Woodstock was about fifteen minutes by car from Oxford and most famous for one thing. "You live in Blenheim Palace?" I'd toured it once. A huge palace built by the Duke of Marlborough and birthplace of Winston Churchill.

He shot me a look. "Too many tourists."

I laughed. "Okay. Surprise me."

I looked out the window, enjoying being out of the shop. As soon as we were out of Oxford we drove past green fields dotted with sheep, some of whose wool would no doubt end up in my shop. I could see the hills of the Cotswolds rising ahead and scatterings of houses made of gray Cotswold stone. We passed three tour buses headed for Blenheim, a group of Lycra-clad cyclists who appeared to be preparing for a race, and countless cars filled with families enjoying a Sunday afternoon drive, perhaps heading to one of the pubs for Sunday lunch.

We drove through the town of Woodstock, with its quaint stone houses, hotels and pubs and out the other side. The road grew much quieter and we turned off into a smaller road with ancient trees that arched overhead. It was so quiet here.

After another five minutes or so, Rafe picked up a key fob as we approached a pair of stone pillars topped with lions that held a black iron gate between them. He pushed a button and the iron gates opened with majestic slowness.

We passed through them and down a private avenue to a grand, stately home. The inner garden was walled and a gardener was at work trimming back the fading hydrangeas. On the velvet, green lawns that bordered the drive, three peacocks pecked at the ground.

Another watched from atop a wall, its green and blue feathers iridescent in the afternoon sunshine. I couldn't believe my eyes. "Peacocks? You have peacocks?" It was somehow easier to focus on the birds than on the palace he called home.

"I do."

As the car cruised past, one of the three pecking peacocks raised its head, looked at us and began to waddle along, trying to keep up. He was not the handsomest of the birds. He was a little on the chubby side and his tail was a sad thing. He was down to one feather, which dragged behind him in the grass as he ran, like a lone water skier behind an oversized speedboat.

When the car drew up in front of the wide steps leading to the house, the bird sped up so it was standing, waiting like a dog when its master returns, when Rafe opened his car door. I wasn't missing this reunion, so I scrambled out and ran around the back of the car to watch.

"Well, Henri, I see you're keeping healthy," Rafe said, using a French accent for the bird's name. He put a hand in his pocket and pulled out some kind of pellet, which he placed on the palm of his hand. When he squatted, the peacock turned a beady eye to me, and I stood absolutely still until he decided I was no threat and leaned forward to eat out of Rafe's hand.

It was in the top ten of the cutest things I'd ever seen. "Why do you call him Henri?"

"He's French. He was raised on a chateau near Toulouse, but his owners fell on hard times, and, when they sold up, they asked me to take him."

I didn't like to be rude, but the bird seemed unhealthily chubby. "Isn't he a little overweight?"

"Oh, dreadfully. Henri has the body of a peacock and the soul of a pig. He'll eat anything, but he's partial to steak." He looked up at me. "He's molting at the moment, which is why he looks so unkempt. Would you like to feed him?"

"Will he let me?"

"I think so." He gestured and I went closer and knelt beside Rafe. Henri sidled back a couple of steps, but when Rafe put the birdseed pellet in my hand, and I held it out flat, the bird's greed quickly overcame his wariness and he waddled forward and quite daintily took the pellet from my palm.

Then, Rafe said, "That's quite enough, Henri. Go and get some exercise."

The bird tossed his head as if to say, 'As if.' Then Henri turned and waddled back, dusting the road with that single tail feather.

When we stood up, Rafe said, "Welcome."

"This place is incredible."

"Thank you. The original house is Tudor. It was quite run down when I bought it. I added the wings on either side in the late seventeen hundreds. Capability Brown planned the garden and grounds." Built of the local stone, the manor was like something you'd visit on a tour, not a place where anyone but a celebrity might live.

The door opened before we'd climbed the stairs and a middle-aged man wearing a blue suit stood waiting. "Good afternoon, miss," he said to me. And to Rafe, "Welcome home."

I mumbled, "Good afternoon," then walked through the doors into a Jane Austen novel. Honestly, that's how I felt. Like Elizabeth when she visits Pemberley. Maybe this house was on a smaller scale, but I got the feeling of wealth, good taste, and history all working together. And I was still only in the foyer. It featured tiled floors with rich carpeting, a grand staircase in the middle and a fireplace big enough to roast an elephant.

The man in blue shut the wide double doors as Rafe said, "Thank you, William."

"Ring when you're ready for lunch." And then the man disappeared.

I stared at Rafe. "Is he Alfred to your Bruce Wayne?"

Rafe looked at me as though I might have a fever. "I beg your pardon?"

"You know, Batman?"

He still looked as though he had no idea what I was talking about. I rolled my eyes. "Has popular American culture completely escaped you?"

"I certainly hope so."

So, tall, dark and undead didn't know everything. I was determined, one day very soon, to get him into a darkened movie theater and expand his cultural education.

As I was thinking of movies and TV shows I wanted him to see, he was leading me off the foyer to the left of the grand staircase. He opened one of a pair of double doors and we walked into a large room with modern, comfortable couches and chairs, a large Georgian fireplace, and a chandelier of epic proportions. But all that was nothing to the paintings grouped on wooden paneled walls.

I nearly swallowed my tongue, which was probably as well as it stopped me from saying something stupid. One entire wall was Monet and the blues and greens were so fresh, the water lilies might have been painted that week. So fresh, I had to ask, "Monet's not a vampire, is he?" Could he still be there? The ghost of Giverny, painting away and selling his work in the literal underground economy.

Rafe looked amused. "If he is, I haven't heard of it."

"You must be a fan of the impressionists," I said, walking around to study a wall of pictures that included two Van Goghs, a few Turners, a Pissarro and some artists I'd never heard of.

"My walls change according to my mood."

When I raised my brows in a silent question, he turned a brass handle at the bottom of a section of paneling, and two panels opened like doors. Behind, was another series of paintings.

I recognized the Rembrandt, had to squint at the signature to get the Van Dyck and when I saw a series of sketches by Da Vinci I nearly had a heart attack. "These are old masters. Do you have any idea what they are worth?"

He came to stand beside me, and we both studied the sketches. "To me, they are priceless, as is the pleasure they've given me over the years. Money becomes meaningless after a while."

I couldn't imagine ever being that blasé about money, but then I couldn't imagine being a vampire, either.

He opened another set of panels to reveal an entire wall of Picasso. "Gertrude Stein and I used to argue about him."

"You and Gertrude Stein. In Paris, in the 1920s?"

"Of course. Her salons were quite remarkable." He smiled, a little sadly. "I miss that crowd. Those were exciting times."

He showed me around the rest of his house and I became more and more intrigued by the man behind the vampire.

His library was, of course, amazing, and, with its double height walls covered floor to ceiling in books, had an elaborate system of ladders and brass rails that they slid along.

Behind the library, was a very modern office with two computers and modern office furniture. The bedrooms were a mix of old and new. New mattresses, bedding and curtains, and mainly antique furniture.

His bedroom was the most modern, with a king-size bed and deep, comfortable chairs. The paint, carpets and bedding were a soothing, cool gray palette. The windows were shuttered so the light was muted. The ensuite bathroom included a large, glassed-in shower with about seventeen shower heads, a sauna and a deep bath tub.

Even if I hadn't known he was an insomniac, I think I would have guessed. Everything in this room was meant to soothe, and from the number of books, I imagined he spent a lot of time reading instead of sleeping.

We had lunch, not in the formal dining room, but in a glass-roofed conservatory. The air smelled of roses and orchids and the glass walls were perfect for keeping out the chill but offering views of the acres of grounds. He even had his own lake, glinting like the pewter surface of my scrying mirror.

I'd never eaten lunch with a vampire before and I was a bit worried about what I'd be served, but William came in with a tray of assorted sandwiches, cold meats, cured salmon and salads.

He offered wine, soft drinks, tea or coffee and I chose sparkling water. I filled my plate, feeling hungry after hiking the acres of this house and figuring I'd better carbo load if I was going to make it around the huge garden. Rafe put a generous helping of the raw salmon on his plate, and some salad. He also drank sparkling water.

"This is so beautiful," I said as we ate. "What do you call it? Crosyer Castle?"

He shook his head. "Woodbridge House, actually. That was the original name and I've kept it. I prefer to remain as anonymous as possible."

I finished my meal with coffee and a delicious lemon cake that William had made himself. Rafe had more water and watched me eat. "I feel terrible that William made this whole cake just for me."

"I think he's happy to have someone to cook for. My meals aren't as interesting to prepare."

I hesitated, then asked, "Does he know?"

"Oh, yes. His family have served me for centuries. Each generation is brought up to it and have remained faithful and discreet. William's sister is the head gardener and his cousin keeps on top of repairs. They all hire extra staff as needed, but between them, the three of them run the place."

"Must be a great place to work."

"I think so. It's where I do most of my work, too."

I pushed my plate away, licking the last of the lemon from my lip.

He reached for my hand and pulled me to my feet. "Come, let's walk outside before it gets cold." And so we did, around the lake, and through a wood. "An ancient right-of-way passes through here," he said, pointing to a well-used footpath. "So it's always open to walkers and horse riders."

"You don't mind?" He seemed such a stickler for privacy.

"There wouldn't be any point in minding. England is covered in public footpaths that cross private land. But, no, I don't mind. I'm happy to share these grounds with those who appreciate them."

We walked back to the house and, when I went to thank William for lunch, I found him in a very modern kitchen, complete with top-of-the-line appliances and granite counter tops. The wood plank floor looked pretty old and outside the window I could see a kitchen garden, bursting with herbs that had probably been planted hundreds of years ago.

"Thank you for lunch, William. It was delicious."

"I'm glad you enjoyed it." And he offered me a basket.

"What's this?"

"Leftover cake. You seemed to enjoy it."

"Oh, but you should have it. You made it."

He shook his head, then patted his belly. "Since Rafe doesn't have a sweet tooth, I'd end up eating all of it. Please, you'll do me a favor if you take it away."

What could I do but accept?

As we drove home, I said, "Thank you."

Rafe looked at me sideways, his lips curving. "For what?"

"For everything, today, but mostly thank you for not even mentioning the murder. It was nice to have a break."

My break didn't last long.

CHAPTER 14

*M*onday morning, I opened as usual.

"May I help you?" I asked the group of ladies who entered my shop. I recognized them as the four women who had taken tea on that fateful day when Colonel Montague died.

Once more, Miss Everly led the group. She looked as well turned out as the last time I'd seen her, this time in a camel coat and heels. Her friends looked as frumpy as the last time I'd seen them. She came forward, "We've always loved this shop, haven't we, girls?"

I loved that she referred to them as girls when they must all be in their seventies or eighties. "I believe it was your grandmother who used to run the place. Agnes Bartlett? Oh, my, that's a lovely photograph of her on the wall. She was such a nice woman. I was very sorry to hear of her passing."

When I'd first taken over the shop, words of condolence had stabbed me in the heart every time. Now that I was aware my grandmother was undead and a sleepwalker, they filled me with trepidation.

It wasn't too bad when strangers or tourists caught sight of a slightly pale and very sleepy looking octogenarian wandering around the shop, but when it was someone who had known her in life... I shuddered. The spell I'd cast on Agatha had saved me once this week, I didn't want to rely on my budding powers any more than I had to. I only hoped my trap door spell held.

I agreed that it was very sad to lose her. And yes, I was her granddaughter, Lucy. The four ladies wandered around the shop as customers did, poking into baskets and flipping through knitting catalogs.

The shoppers in Cardinal Woolsey's came in two categories. There were browsers and there were buyers. Most buyers came in with a specific project in mind or a general idea of what they wanted. For instance, "I want to make a thick, warm sweater for my grandson. His favorite color is blue." Or, "My daughter's expecting. It's my first grandchild, I've been looking forward to knitting baby's first sweater since I learned to knit. I suppose I'll have to do something in yellow or green since we don't know the sex."

The browsers on the other hand, wandered around with their gazes flitting from one thing to another. Sometimes they might buy on impulse, but usually they were killing time. These four seemed like browsers.

Of course, the fun for me was trying to turn browsers into buyers.

Miss Everly, after making a pretense of studying Icelandic sweaters suddenly put down the book. "I believe I saw you in the tea shop. When poor Colonel Montague passed away."

I nodded. "That's right. It was a terrible shock."

"I knew him, you know."

Oh, I knew all about her history with the colonel. But, since she only knew me as young Lucy from across the pond, she wouldn't have any idea of the information my grandmother had passed on to me. I looked politely interested. "How sad for you to lose a friend."

She glanced at me strangely and I wondered if I'd put too much emphasis on the word friend. "I've been racking my brains to think who would want to wish the colonel harm. Although I was sitting closer to him than you were, I had my back to him. But you had quite a good view, didn't you?"

Was she doing her own amateur sleuthing? Did she really wonder if I might have extra information? Or was she checking to see whether I might be able to implicate her? I had no way of knowing, but I told the truth. "I probably had a better view of the colonel's table than you did, but I was having a conversation with my friend. I really didn't see much of what went on."

"There was that very unfortunate incident when he was served the wrong tea. I can't help wondering whether the tea was meant for someone else?"

One of her three friends giggled nervously over the crochet hooks. "Why, then, any of us could have been the intended victim. Makes one wonder, doesn't it?"

"But couldn't the poisoning have been accidental? Some kind of food poisoning?"

Miss Everly shook her head. "I was a biochemist. The symptoms were all wrong. No, he was poisoned deliberately."

I looked at them all, so seemingly innocent. Four kindly old ladies who'd only wanted a quiet cup of tea after their friend's funeral and had become embroiled in such a horrible death.

And yet, I am not fooled by old ladies. My grandmother and her friend Sylvia have two of the sharpest minds I know. I looked at them. "Do you have enemies?" It seemed to me that people who got murdered generally had enemies who wanted them dead.

Miss Everly said something very surprising. "I imagine we all have enemies. It's a question of knowing how far they will go."

I was relieved when the door opened and a young mother came in pushing a pram containing a sleeping baby. Naturally, the four ladies all went into grandmother mode and cooed over the sleeping child. The tired looking mother glanced at me. "Do you have any patterns for baby blankets?"

This woman was a shopper. I didn't know how long that baby would keep sleeping but I suspected the woman timed her shopping expeditions precisely to the length of the nap. I'd better be snappy if I didn't want to lose the sale or have a screaming baby on my hands. I took her immediately to the patterns and leaflets and picked out three fairly simple blanket patterns, one slightly more complicated and an advanced pattern.

She picked an easy one out of my hand, then looked at me in bewilderment. "I don't know what to do with myself. I used to be a banker, with a team of eight employees. I had my nails done weekly and went on business trips to Zurich, Frankfurt and Paris. Now, I barely have time to shower. The baby finally goes to sleep and I'm so tired I want something mindless to do with my hands."

She wasn't a walking advertisement for motherhood, that

was for sure. The poor mother looked absolutely exhausted, with dark circles under her eyes and clothes spattered with milk and what looked like baby spit up.

"This pattern won't be very taxing on your brain." And then I offered her a selection of yarns that would be appropriate. She picked several colors almost at random and thanked me. I rang up her purchases and she tucked them into the basket of the pram just as mewling noises emerged from the baby.

She turned the pram toward the door when a sound like a baby seagull crying emerged from the pram. The mother moaned in despair. I soon saw why. After a couple of experimental seagull cries the child broke out screaming. I would not have believed any creature that small could make so much noise.

"My, that's a healthy pair of lungs," one of Miss Everly's friends said, taking a step back. Mother looked like she was going to start screaming herself. She said, "I just want a little peace and quiet. I want to knit, is that too much to ask? Half an hour of peace and quiet so I can knit?"

At that moment Sylvia came in the front door. She was carrying a shopping bag from the most expensive shoe shop in Oxford. She nodded politely to the ladies and then, pretending to be a shopper, began to look aimlessly into the various baskets.

I felt the distress coming from the poor new mother and from the baby. I came out from behind my counter and walked forward. "May I? I've always been good with babies."

I didn't even wait for the mother's approval. I leaned down and picked up the squalling baby. He was a little boy all in blue except for the red on his face. Bright red. He was screaming so loud he could barely draw enough breath before he started screaming again. I held him like a football and looked down into his eyes, so blue, so confused, so angry. He opened them wide and stared right into mine.

I leaned in close and murmured, "I know it's going to seem strange at first, but this is a good place and you get used to it."

He took another breath but he didn't scream quite so loud this time. He looked at me, puzzled, as though perhaps we'd met before but he couldn't remember where. I smiled down at him. I could smell his lovely baby smell and feel the warmth of his little body curled into mine. I began to rock in an ancient rhythm that I don't think any woman ever learns, perhaps rocking is passed down in our genes. He began to breathe with my rhythm and then drifted back to sleep again.

I said to the new mom, who still jangled with stress. "Sit in that chair and knit for a little while. I'll hold your baby."

She nodded and did as I said. One of the old ladies looked at me. "It's like you have a magic with children."

I stared at her. Ever since I was a kid and started babysitting I'd been able to settle children. Had I been using magic without even knowing it?

The four ladies sighed blissfully as the baby and I rocked. One of the frumpy friends said, "I miss my daughter and my grandchildren. I know you asked us to stay, Gina, but I really think I'll take the train home to Warwick tomorrow."

Her friend agreed that she would also like to leave. I thought Miss Everly looked less than pleased by this abandonment. There was only the verger left to support her and I suspected she was busy being a verger.

"Why don't you come with us? There's nothing you can do here."

Miss Everly shook her head. "I can't leave. Someone must support the colonel's wife. Poor, dear Elspeth."

I wondered if the poor colonel's wife had any interest in being comforted by the woman who had once been in love with her husband and suspected the answer was no. I was fairly certain my opinion coincided with that of the other three. They glanced among themselves looking disapproving. I wondered if it was nosiness keeping Miss Everly in Oxford and she'd be better to get on the train and go home.

However, I kept my forthright American opinions to myself.

One of them said, "All this shopping is making me tired. I'd dearly love a cup of tea. What a shame the tea shop is closed." She gave a gasp, realizing how insensitive she sounded, and fell over herself trying to explain that she hadn't meant that the shop should reopen. But what a shame there wasn't another tea shop close by and then she looked at me. "At least, it's been such a long time since I lived in Oxford. Perhaps there is another tea shop nearby?"

There were a couple of coffee shop chain stores on High Street, as I'm sure they knew, but I directed them there and the four of them left.

Once they were gone, Sylvia fetched a chair from the back and sat beside the overwhelmed mother. The pair of them sat side-by-side knitting contentedly. I settled into my chair behind my desk holding the baby against me, his warm breath against my neck and his tiny hands clutching my blouse. It was a very pleasant half hour.

The mother looked at her cell phone. "I must go. But

thank you. I don't think I could have coped for one more minute."

I had no worldly advice to give her. All I could offer was the chance to bring her baby anytime she needed a break.

When she left, Sylvia said, "You've been practicing your magic I see. Your grandmother will be pleased."

"I've had this ability forever. I never knew it was special."

She smiled. "A great deal of magic is simply drawing from the natural world, and communicating at a deeper level. That's what you were doing with that child, wasn't it?"

"Yes, I think it was."

"I'm enjoying watching your powers strengthen. I wonder where you'll end up?"

I wondered that myself, some days it all seemed over-whelming.

CHAPTER 15

I was reading the surprisingly glowing report on Katie from Australia when Rafe appeared like a puff of black smoke at my elbow. He didn't actually materialize, but he was so soft-footed and untroubled by doors and locks that it always appeared that way to me. He said, "You're looking serious."

"Not serious, puzzled. Katie, aka Katya, is a terrible waitress but an excellent knitter."

"It's good to have a hobby in jail. Helps pass the time."

That's probably why I was looking serious. "I don't think she is a killer. And, furthermore, Nyx likes her."

Nyx was currently rubbing herself against his legs and he looked down. "Nyx is a very poor judge of character." Then he picked the cat up. She crawled up and over his shoulder and hung there like a sack of grain, if grain could purr.

"I'm thinking about hiring Katie."

"Why?"

"Because she can knit, and she has an excellent reference

from a previous knitting shop. She took that tangle I'd made and turned it into an actual sock. It was magic."

He looked unimpressed. "Perhaps it was magic. Maybe she's one of your sisters?"

I stared at him. "There are spells to untangle knitting?" Why had that never occurred to me? That heavy, ornate grimoire was full of love spells and forgetfulness spells, spells for finding lost items and many ways to curse your enemies, but I didn't recall seeing anything about untangling botched knitting. If I'd known I could've used magic I would have done.

"Ask your grandmother, I'm sure it's possible."

I felt my mouth take on the shape of a pout. "Gran never told me about such a spell."

"I suspect it's because she wants you to learn how to knit."

"She was much nicer when she was alive." It wasn't true, but I was enjoying my pout.

"We know so little about Katie, Lucy, she could well turn out to be a murderer."

I didn't think she had any reason to murder me, but then she didn't seem to have a reason to kill the colonel, either. "She did let drop a very interesting piece of information. There was rat poison in the kitchen."

"I'm no expert, but I don't think that will turn out to be the poison. First it's got a very strong flavor. Tea wouldn't be enough to mask it. And the victim would take longer to die."

I really didn't want to dwell on that mental picture. "I keep wondering who would want Colonel Montague dead."

"I've been asking around. The old boy'd been acting irrationally. Possibly from dementia. Until the autopsy's completed it will be impossible to say what disease he suffered from. It could be Alzheimer's, Parkinson's, even bipolar, but he'd taken to spending vast sums of money on extremely peculiar purchases. He bought a racehorse with no background in racing. Then a vintage Aston Martin and he was talking about buying property in Ibiza. The man didn't even like travel."

"Could he have mixed up his medication somehow and poisoned himself?"

"No. Sorry, Lucy. I wish, for your sake, I could spin this as an accident, but he was definitely murdered. I had a look at his sons. Neither of them are well-to-do. Perhaps they were protecting their inheritance."

"What about the wife?"

"She'd have the same motive. But her grief and shock seemed so genuine, I'm not sure anyone's that good an actress."

I had to agree. She'd seemed ill with grief.

I told him about Miss Everly and her visit to my shop. "I don't know why she wants to stay. Does she really want to comfort the widow? The woman who married the man she loved?"

"Who can say?"

"But did she kill him? Finally getting her revenge after all these years. Maybe she can't leave the scene of the crime. She's never murdered anyone before and she's fascinated by the aftermath. Too much so to resume her dull life."

"Killing a man isn't as exciting as you seem to think it is," he said drily. No doubt he knew from experience, and I did not want the details.

"Do you think it's impossible?"

He treated me to his truly charming smile. "I think your

theory is a little far-fetched. But if Miss Everly invites you for tea, I suggest you decline the invitation."

My half hour of rocking the child have given me time to think and I decided to give Katie a job. Sure, she might be a murderer, but I wanted to give her the benefit of the doubt. Just as I hoped she'd give me the benefit of the doubt if she ever discovered I was a witch.

And our downstairs neighbors were all vampires.

I was watching as yet another young woman, walking by the shop, stopped and did a double-take, then pulled out her cell phone and snapped a picture of Nyx, lounging in the bowl of colored wool. Since I could never sell the stuff she'd slept in, I'd taken to putting stray wool in the bowl. As the woman posted the picture, I decided to put our shop brochures in the window beside the bowl so anyone posting photos of the cat in the shop window would be advertising Cardinal Woolsey's. "I should put you on payroll," I told Nyx as I positioned the brochures strategically around her. She opened one eye, and then rolled over, exposing her belly and looking even cuter. As I was patting her, I noticed Florence Watt and Gerald Pettigrew stroll by arm in arm. That romance hadn't faltered, in spite of Mary Watt's hostility and the murder.

They saw me and waved, cheerily. I waved back, thinking how nice it was to see them so happy together.

Between customers, I put together a few sweater kits, something Gran had taught me to do. I took a pattern and collected all the supplies necessary, then packaged the set. It saved the customer time and trouble.

I also checked for special orders. We shipped worldwide and I noticed there was an order from Scotland and another from Canada. I was collecting the wools when another order came in. This one local, with delivery requested. We delivered within Oxford if the customer was unable to come to the store for some reason, mainly as a courtesy. We didn't charge much and I would either run the order over on my bicycle, or brave the traffic in Gran's little car.

Fortunately, this order was near enough that I could bike, but when I read it through carefully, my eyes widened. It was from Elspeth Montague. I doubted there were many Elspeth Montagues in Oxford, and Gran had said she'd been a customer in earlier times. Was it possible the colonel's wife was taking up knitting, once again?

After all our stratagems for gaining entry to her home, here she was asking me to go to her.

I filled all three orders, and, as soon as the shop closed, I put on my coat and took Elspeth Montague's parcel. The others I'd put in the post tomorrow.

It was chilly outside as I got on my bike and headed to St. John Street. The homes there were terraced, Georgian gentility. Many had been broken up into student housing, but the house I found myself in front of still looked to be intact. I rang the bell, wondering what I should say or do, when the door opened and Elspeth Montague stood there.

The worst of her grief seemed to have passed, but she still looked pale and shaken. When she saw the Cardinal Woolsey's bag, she smiled at me in what looked like relief. "Oh, thank you, dear. I've been beside myself for the past few days and suddenly thought how nice it would be to have a project. I can't concentrate on anything, you see. Not the television, not a book. But knitting is so soothing, isn't it?"

"Yes. For some people it really is." I was not one of them,

but this was neither the time nor the place for such a disclosure.

I'd planned to ask subtle questions about the murder, but I found I couldn't. All that came out of my mouth was, "How are you?"

She seemed startled by the question and looked at me more closely. Then she nodded. "You were there. Weren't you?"

"Yes. I'm so very sorry."

"He was never an easy man, my husband, but one is suddenly so lost without him."

I was nearly convinced that we could cross Elspeth off the list of possible murderers, but what of the rest of the family? "How are your children taking the tragedy?"

Once more, she looked startled, and I supposed most people were too delicate to ask such direct questions. Especially strange delivery people who'd arrived by bicycle. "As well as can be expected." Then she pressed her lips together as though trying not to cry. "The truth is, I think they're relieved. It's an awful thing to say, I know, but he wasn't a very nice father." She gasped, then, and almost grabbed the bag out of my hands. "Perhaps he wasn't a very nice man."

I didn't know what to say. I couldn't agree with her, but I wasn't going to contradict her, as everything I'd heard about the man suggested he was a nasty old codger.

"You charged my credit card, I think."

"Yes. Thank you. It's all taken care of. I hope you enjoy knitting that sweater."

"I think it will soothe me. Thank you for bringing it to me. I can't quite face going out, yet. People stare at one so."

"Let me know if there's anything else you need."

She nodded, thanked me again, and shut the door. I wheeled my bike around and then nearly fell off it when I saw the Irish woman who'd been in the tea shop when the colonel was murdered walking toward me. She might not have noticed me if I hadn't nearly fallen, but when she glanced at my face, she jumped like a scared rabbit, and turned around and began briskly walking back the way she'd come.

Did she think I hadn't recognized her? Or that I didn't want to talk to the woman who'd nearly had me arrested? I took after her on my bike. It wasn't much of a contest. No matter how fast she walked, I was clearly going to overtake her. We had a ridiculous kind of race, where she walked faster and faster and I kept pace with her on my bike. We roared up St. John Street to Wellington Square, which was one of those hidden green spaces that were usually a delight to come upon.

We speed-walked and cycled around the wrought iron fence surrounding the green space until there was an opening and she darted into the fenced garden. Since she was as good as entering a cage, I assumed she planned to stop running. I got off my bike and wheeled it into the gated park. There was no one else there on a chilly October evening at dusk. She walked ahead, catching her breath and I followed her to a wooden bench beneath a tree. I settled my bike against the bench and faced her, with my hands on my hips. I remembered the humiliation of being carted off in the back of a police car and was not feeling warm and fuzzy toward this woman.

"You slipped that newspaper article into my bag, didn't you?"

She didn't answer. She was breathing hard and had a hand to her chest.

I didn't even think about how she might have killed a man and tried to frame me, and that, perhaps, telling her off here in a deserted park wasn't the smartest thing I'd ever done. I was too mad to think clearly. "You'd better tell me exactly what you were doing in that tea shop and why you had that newspaper cutting. And it better be the truth."

She sat on the bench, quite suddenly. "I was planning to confront him," she said, panting. "The colonel."

I was not impressed. "Confront? Or kill?"

She shook her head. Then dug into the pocket of her camel coat. I flinched, wondering if she had something lethal in there, but she pulled out a pack of tissues and then blew her nose. Her cheeks were pink with the cold, or the exercise, maybe both. "I'd planned to confront him in public, in front of his wife. I swear to you, that's all I was going to do. I was watching him, trying to get up my courage, when he fell ill."

I thought of the articles I'd read about the colonel. "Did he kill someone you loved?"

She gave an unpleasant, jeering laugh. "Quite the opposite."

I'd been on my feet most of the day, I was tired, it was cold, and I didn't feel like playing games. "What?"

She put the tissues away and rested her hands in her lap. She had on gloves. I wished I'd thought to bring some. "He caused someone I love very much to be born."

I felt my eyes pop open; now, even my eyeballs were getting cold. "You had an affair with Colonel Montague?"

"Not me. My sister." She shook her head. "Foolish, romantic, Eileen. She came in daily to cook for him, you see. I think she really believed he'd be delighted when she found out she was expecting. Quite the opposite, of course. He was furious. Accused her of trying to trap him and acted like she was the one who'd done wrong. He fired her on the spot and wouldn't have anything to do with her, or the babe."

I was sorry anyone had died the way the colonel had, but he really did seem like he'd been a bad man.

She shook her head, sadly. "Those were different times. Our da said she'd betrayed her own people, going with an Englishman. Her friends weren't much better. In the end, she left and moved to England. She kept the baby, to her credit. My niece, Sharon, is a wonderful woman. I've had her with me often, to give her mum a rest. But now my sister's ill. Overwork and worry, never having enough money, have worn her out. I wanted to tell that awful man what he'd done, and demand he support the woman whose life he so nearly ruined."

It was a glib story, but I wasn't convinced. A woman who would frame an innocent woman, like me, wasn't completely trustworthy.

No doubt she could read my doubts, even in the fading light, for she stood and faced me squarely. "I panicked when he died like that. I'd planned to push that article in his face, and tell him what I thought of him. I had photographs of the child to show his wife. But, I didn't kill him, and when they said we had to go across the road, and turn out our pockets and handbags, I slipped the newspaper into your bag when no one was looking. You'd gone to make a phone call and it was done in the twinkle of an eye."

Maybe a twinkle of her eye. "They took me to the police station and questioned me."

Her gaze sank, so she was looking somewhere near my knees. "I'm sorry for that. It was wrong of me. And cowardly." She took a deep breath. "Shall I tell the police? Get you out of trouble?"

I was tempted, but I shook my head. "They believed me that it wasn't mine. I think they may be looking for you, though, to help with their enquiries. You might be wise to tell them what you've told me."

She bit her lip, then nodded. "I must see the colonel's wife, first. Then, when I've done that, I'll go to the police."

"You're not going to tell that poor, grieving widow that her husband was unfaithful, are you?"

Her head came up at that and her eyes burned into mine. "Indeed, I am. She's a right to know, and his daughter has a right to an inheritance. Her life has been so poor, you see. She's had none of the advantages he should have provided her. Now, she's a woman in her forties and she's looking after her mother. They deserve that he should provide for them, even if it's from the grave."

"Oh, poor Elspeth," I said.

"Better it come from me, quietly, than from a solicitor."

"Can you prove he's the father?"

She gave another of those jeering laughs. "He wrote her letters, including one where he accuses her of trying to trap him into marriage. But we must demand a DNA test, before he's buried, so you see it's quite urgent."

"Well, try not to upset her too much."

Poor Elspeth.

And poor Eileen and her daughter.

I thought Elspeth was going to need her soothing knitting more than she'd imagined.

CHAPTER 16

*W*hen Katie arrived for her first shift the next day, she impressed me immediately by showing up ten minutes early. She carried a brown paper bag, which I had assumed was her lunch until she presented it to me. "Surprise."

I looked in the bag and there were my socks. Well, not my socks. Nothing resembling the mess I'd made. This was a pair of perfect socks.

"I can't believe you knit those so fast." I immediately pulled off my shoes and slipped the socks on my feet. "And they fit perfectly," I said, wiggling my toes in the warm, woolly socks.

"I measured them against my own feet, thinking we were about the same size." She looked as pleased as I felt and I hoped this meant we were off to a good start.

Katie needed very little training, since she knew a lot more about knitting than I did, and seemed very conversant with the various wools and supplies. She didn't even need much training on the cash register as she'd used a similar one at her last job.

When we had a quiet lull with no customers, I said, "How is Jim doing?"

"Great," was the surprising reply. "He got a part in a play. Of course, it's only community, and it doesn't pay, but he's stoked because it gives him something to do. Even though our names haven't been in the papers, everybody in the food trade knows everybody else in Oxford. He's got no hope of being hired anywhere, and, of course, we couldn't leave if we wanted to until this is all cleared up."

"Oh, I'm so sorry." And very glad I was doing my bit by giving her this job.

"Miss Watt came by with some money and told us how sorry she was things had turned out this way. We thought it was very decent of her."

It was indeed decent. Could she be feeling guilty? I shook my head. I had to stop seeing guilty motives everywhere. Mary Watt was a lovely woman. She'd only wanted to help two employees who'd become embroiled in a very unfortunate event. Of course she hadn't killed Colonel Montague. But then, who had? It seemed like loads of people had reason to hate the man and none had harmed him. Except, of course, that someone had.

CHAPTER 17

By lunch time, I was feeling quite pleased with my decision to hire Katie. She had a knack for selling. She wasn't pushy at all, but, because she was such a good knitter herself, she was a lot more help to customers than I was. She could reassure them that they could indeed manage whatever project they were mulling over and, unlike Agatha, she didn't despise our customers, which was a good thing.

She seemed to take a keen interest in their projects and helped answer tricky questions like whether this woman's grandson, who was about her age, would prefer green or blue, chunky textured wool or smooth. Naturally, the customers felt more confident when she had approved their instincts or guided them gently to better choices. I wondered if our visitors thought it was odd that this quintessentially English shop was being run by an American and an Australian, but no one said a word, at least not to our faces.

Any fears I'd had that the tea shop next door being closed

would affect business were soon discarded. In fact, after the first couple of days, we were as busy as ever.

More than one person came up to me looking hopeful. "Isn't it a terrible shame about the tragedy next door?"

I muttered soothingly and noncommittally. I didn't wish to gossip about the tragedy and I was keenly aware that Katie was, as far as I knew, a suspect. My bland politeness discouraged most of the nosy parkers. Katie was even more blunt. The couple of people who asked her searching questions got a blank stare and, "I'm Australian. I only started working here today."

I had to hand it to her. She hadn't lied, she'd just left out the part where she'd been working at Elderflower the day the colonel died.

I was thinking about telling Katie she could go for lunch when a woman in her late thirties came in. She had dark hair cropped short, and was wearing khaki trousers, a T-shirt, and a sweater that had come from a department store and certainly never been hand-knit. She glanced around the shop, and I went forward. I gave my standard greeting. "Good morning. Let us know if we can help you."

"Thank you. I'll just have a wander."

She seemed to me not to be shopping so much as killing time and I was proved correct when the two customers in the shop had paid up and left. Now there was only Katie, me and the stranger. The woman made her way over to me. "Do you have anything for a beginner?"

I suggested a simple scarf. We even had some patterns we gave away for free, full of instructions. "Oh yes. Very nice." Then she said, "I heard about the death next door at the tea shop. Isn't it terrible?"

I agreed that it was terrible and then tried to bring the conversation back to knitting, but she was having none of it. "I understand you were there. My aunt and uncle were in the tea shop when it happened, you see, and they're very shaken up about it. My aunt recognized you from the shop. They live not too far from here." She made a vague gesture with her hand. "My aunt is so frightened that there's a murderer on the loose that she can't sleep. It must be terrible for you, being right next door."

Was this woman simply a ghoul? Was she trying to pump me for information? What did she think I knew? "I'm very sorry for your aunt and uncle. Yes, it was terrible."

"I think what makes it worse is that she really didn't see anything. She said that you had a very good view of the death."

Her words brought vivid memories back again and I felt as though I were once more watching Colonel Montague in his death throes. I must've shuddered. "Your aunt could have had my seat and welcome. I don't have any idea who killed him, if that's what your aunt wants to know. If I had I would've told the police right away."

"Of course you would. It's just that it's funny. Sometimes we don't realize everything we've seen. My aunt said that there were people walking back and forth and I wondered if you might've seen more than you're aware of. Perhaps it would help you to talk it through?"

I didn't like the way the woman was looking at me. This wasn't an idle conversation—she was grilling me. I said, "Really, I'm trying to forget what happened, as much as I can."

That wasn't true of course. I couldn't stop thinking about

the poisoning and what I'd seen. I had as much interest in getting a murderer off the streets as anyone else, especially as they had done their terrible deed right next door to my shop and home. I certainly didn't need some strange woman coming off the street and trying to interrogate me.

Obviously realizing she wasn't going to get me to talk, she said, "There was a young couple working there, a chef and waitress. I heard they were brother and sister. You don't know what happened to them, do you?"

From the corner of my eye I saw Katie go rigid, but I studiously kept my gaze on the woman's face. "Why would I know?"

She was all smiles. "Oh, no reason, except that my aunt tells me Cardinal Woolsey's is the heart of Harrington Street. She says everyone comes through here. I thought perhaps you might've heard."

I hadn't run the shop long shop long enough to know how to get rid of people. I wanted to send this dreadful woman out with a flea in her ear. I thought of that ridiculous phrase, the customer is always right, and how in this case the customer was rude, intrusive, and completely inappropriate. Also, it was very clear she had no intention of buying anything.

I tried to think of something to say that would get rid of her without sounding too rude when, fortunately, an older couple walked into the shop. Even more fortuitously, I recognized them. It was a nice lady I had helped the week before while her patient husband had sat in the visitor's chair gently dozing. I even remembered their names. "Mr. and Mrs. Fotheringham. How are you today? Have you started work on that sweater for your granddaughter?"

You'd have thought I had a memory like a genius, remembering their names and what they'd bought, but I was beginning to recognize my customers, especially nice people like these.

Mrs. Fotheringham beamed at me. She was clearly pleased that I had remembered her. She said, "Bless you, my dear. I think it's going to be lovely. The pale pink was a perfect choice. And can't you just see the puff sleeves with her baby pudgy arms? I showed my daughter and she wants me to knit a matching sweater. So I thought I'd better come in while you've still got lots of wool."

"Of course," I said. "Let me help you." The woman didn't need my help, she knew exactly where the wool was and had a better idea of how many balls of the stuff she needed than I would, but I didn't want to give the rude woman an excuse to stand there chatting to me and, to my absolute delight, I heard the door chime and when I turned, she was leaving.

Later, I recounted the story to my grandmother and Sylvia. They both stared at me as though I was particularly stupid. Gran said, "You have magic, dear. Use it."

"You mean, there's a spell for making people go away?"

"Hundreds of them I should think. You can make them go away permanently, fill their minds with the idea that they left a pot on the stove so they'll run home and check. You could put an invisibility spell on the entire shop so that the woman can never find it again. Unless, of course, you'd like to do away with her permanently? Those spells are a little trickier."

"No. No," I said. "Not permanently. We've had enough of getting rid of people permanently around here. I wonder who she was?" I described her to the two vampires, but neither seemed to recognize the description. I told them about the story of the aunt and uncle but they both agreed with me that it sounded like nonsense.

"Perhaps she's a journalist?"

I hadn't thought of that. "But wouldn't she have told me? For all she knows, I'm one of those people who love to see their names in the paper or their pictures on TV."

They both shook their heads. "Rafe might know."

I found it constantly irritating that these two referred everything to Rafe. If our local vampires had a mayor, it was him. He seemed to be consulted on everything. His opinion held more weight than anyone else's and whatever he decreed, they all rushed around to do his bidding. I found it thoroughly irritating.

I was even irritated that I'd asked him to go with me to Elderflower that day of the murder. He'd ended up being right on the spot of the crime. Which was foolish of me, because he was someone I could talk it through endlessly and he'd noticed things I hadn't. Not that any of this putting our heads together had helped us solve the murder.

After the rude woman left, taking her story about her aunt and uncle with her, and Katie and I were alone in the shop again, I could see that her jaw was clenched and her shoulders up around her ears. I said, "Why don't you go for lunch, now. Get something to eat, maybe take a walk, have a few cigarettes if you need them, but eat a peppermint or something before you come back, would you?" I did not want the place smelling of cigarette smoke.

She hadn't been gone long, when Mary Watt came in the shop. My surprise must have shown on my face. I don't think I'd ever seen her in Cardinal Woolsey's before. "Miss Watt. How nice to see you." I was naturally tempted to ask her how she was doing or how the investigation was coming along, but, having been grilled myself so unpleasantly, I decided to refrain from asking my neighbor impertinent questions. If she wanted to talk about the murder, she would.

It turned out my reticence was unnecessary. She did want to talk about the murder, and she did. At length.

First she ranted at the general unfairness of it all. "If someone wanted that dreadful man dead, couldn't they have found somewhere else to do it? Why pick our tea shop? It's always been a lovely, happy place, and now will be forever associated with murder. I'm not sure we can ever open again. That's assuming that Florence and I manage to stay out of jail."

I tried to think of something soothing to say, but all I could manage was, "I'm so sorry."

She paced up and down, rubbing her work-roughened hands up and down her arms, from elbow to shoulder, over and over. "I haven't knitted in years. Who has time, when running a busy tea shop six days a week? Elderflower's been my life, mine and Flo's. And now, all I can think about is that terrible murder that happened right under our noses.

She paced some more. "Without the shop to run, the days are so long. What do people do who don't have businesses to run? You know what they say, 'the devil makes work for idle hands.' Well I've got no intention of letting my hands be idle." She stopped and turned to me. "I've decided I'll take up knitting again. At least it will give me something to do."

"Do you have any idea when the police will finish their investigation?" Being beside Elderflower I knew that official-looking types were still turning up regularly. I'd seen Ian Chisholm a couple of times and once he saw me watching and waved to me. He hadn't come next door to see how I was, though.

Mary began to wander around the shop but it was more like military pacing than a customer browsing. "I can't even read a book. I can't concentrate. My mind's a complete mess. And television? I can't watch the news. I dread to see our poor tea shop shown on television as the site of a murder. And other than the news, all I ever seem to find is a mystery program on television. Do you think I want to watch a murder mystery? I want someone to solve this one."

I made soothing noises and fairly useless comments of the, 'I'm so sorry' variety, but I don't think she heard them. She was really here to pour out her troubles.

I let her go on for a bit and when there was a pause I told her, not wanting her to find out any other way, that I had hired Katie as my shop assistant. She seemed a little startled. "Is that wise, dear? You know she could be a murderer."

"I know she could be, but somehow I don't think so. And she's an excellent knitter." I pointed to my feet. "She knit me these lovely socks."

Mary looked critically at my feet and nodded. "She's certainly a better knitter than a waitress."

"I think that goes without saying."

Then I said, keeping my eyes on the window so I could see Katie before she came in, "I keep thinking about that day and how poor Katie kept getting all the orders mixed up. She couldn't seem to tell the tables apart. Do you think it's possible that the colonel wasn't the intended victim?"

Mary picked up a ball of fishermen's yarn and then put it back down again. "I don't know. I suppose anything is possible. But if what you're saying is true then the poison had to be on the tray when Katie delivered it to the wrong table. Already in the tea or in the jam or baked into the scone or wherever it was."

I was thinking. "Did a very odd young woman come and visit you today? I described the woman who had asked me all those searching questions. Mary said, "The private investigator, you mean?"

My eyes widened. "She's a private investigator?"

"Well that's what she told us. Colonel Montague's widow hired her."

My first thought was that Mrs. Montague had wasted her money. I had never seen a less subtle investigator or one to whom I was less likely to tell my secrets. "Why would she do that? Doesn't she think the police will find the killer?"

"If you ask me, she's making sure they don't arrest her."

"Why would anyone arrest Mrs. Montague?" I remembered her terrible keening sound when it was clear her husband was dead. I'd caught a glimpse of her face and it had looked less lifelike than her dead husband's. She was like a statue of grief. And even yesterday, when I'd taken her the knitting, she'd seemed so lost and sad.

"Because the colonel wanted to divorce her."

"What?"

For the first time since she'd entered Cardinal Woolsey's, Mary Watt looked slightly cheerful. Imparting a juicy bit of gossip to someone who's not expecting it can do that to a woman. "Oh yes."

"They'd both looked so old. I was always shocked when old people got divorced, but, Gran always said, youthful human passions outlived youth.

"But why?"

She raised her eyebrows. "The usual reason why a silly old fool leaves a wife of half a century."

"He had another woman."

She shrugged her shoulders. "That was the rumor."

"But can anyone confirm this? Do we know who the other woman was?"

"A biochemist. She was an old flame of his, in fact. A Miss Everly?"

It was one thing for a silly old man to dump his wife for a younger model, but he'd chosen woman of the same age. That made him slightly less despicable. "To think of rekindling a romance from half a lifetime ago."

Miss Watt's lips thinned into an angry line. "There's a lot of that going around."

Only then did I realize how tactless I'd been. Of course, her own sister was currently indulging in a similar late life romance with a man she had met in her youth.

"It's so good to be able to talk to you, Lucy. There's no point trying to talk to Florence. My foolish sister has her head in the clouds. Oh, I can't tell you how much I miss your grandmother. I used to pop into the shop and tell her my problems, and she could always pop next door to the tea shop and tell me hers. I miss her dreadfully."

I couldn't agree, of course, because I saw my grandmother daily. Instead, I said, "I'm not Gran, but as soon Katie gets back, why don't we go upstairs and, for a change, I'll make you a cup of tea."

She brightened immediately. "Oh, if you're sure it wouldn't be too much trouble. I'd love that."

Since I thought it might be slightly awkward for her and

Katie to have a conversation, I suggested she go on upstairs and wait for me, and as soon as Katie was back, I'd follow her.

Katie, clearly on her best behavior, returned from lunch before her hour was up. I was pleased to see that she smelled of peppermint, not cigarette smoke. She seemed calmer. She'd gone home for lunch, she told me, and Jim had been there. He'd cooked her lunch and made her laugh and I could see the break had done her the world of good.

I told her I had a friend upstairs and that I was going to take my own lunch hour. "Just bang on the connecting door if you need me."

When I arrived upstairs, Mary Watt was standing, looking listlessly out the window. She couldn't keep her hands still but kept rubbing them together and playing with her rings.

Gran's knitting basket was sitting beside the couch. It was an old one, from before she died, as these days she carried her current project around in a tapestry bag. I retrieved the basket and told Mary to take whatever she wanted. I didn't think Gran had many patterns up here but I could easily slip downstairs and find one.

"Oh no, don't bother with a pattern. I couldn't follow it. I'll just make something simple. A scarf, I think. She turned over some of the random balls of wool in the basket and nodded. "I can use up some of these bits and pieces to make a nice striped scarf. It's a thrifty way to use up old wool." She seemed relieved to have a project, even if it was just using up old scraps of wool.

"Well, I'll get the tea on then."

By the time I returned from the kitchen with a pot of good, strong English tea, a plate of cheese sandwiches, and biscuits, she was already busy at work. She seemed calmer, now her hands were occupied.

She'd begun with a row of red. I recognized the wool. Gran had made me a cherry red sweater out of it, which she'd given me just last Christmas.

"Do you know, Lucy, this is the first time I've felt relaxed since that poor man keeled over dead in my tea shop."

I poured our tea and settled back with mine. Nyx had followed me and, after a lunchtime snack of her own, jumped up and settled in my lap.

Mary Watt put down the knitting when I offered her a sandwich. "This is the first food I've fancied today. A murder in one's tea shop is as good as a slimming diet."

"I think there's more on your mind than poor Colonel Montague." I gave her the opening and it was up to her if she wanted to talk further about her troubles. I didn't want to pry, but sometimes just being able to talk about troubles halved them, or so Gran liked to say.

Mary Watt regarded me over the top of her flowered teacup. "You're very like your grandmother, aren't you? She was a perceptive woman and you're growing to be very like her."

"There isn't a greater compliment you could pay me."

"You're right, of course. I was troubled well before the murder. It's Flo, you see."

She picked up her knitting again and as she began to talk, the stitches seemed to fly from one needle to the other as though keeping pace with the torrent of words. "And that *awful* Gerald Pettigrew."

I had thought that was the source of the problem. I nodded.

"Florence thinks I'm a jealous old cow, but that's not it. If she can be bothered to take on an old man at her time of life, more power to her." She raised her gaze to mine and I could see how troubled she was. "But not Gerald Pettigrew."

She finished one row and immediately flipped the needles and began another. "I don't know how the man's got the gall to come back here. I thought I'd got rid of him once and for all. But he's a sly old devil, and he knows he's got me." She dropped the knitting to her lap and turned to me. "Oh, whatever am I going to do?"

Since I couldn't make head nor tail of what she was talking about, I kept my mouth closed and looked at her with sympathy.

She sighed and picked up her knitting again. "You must think I'm a lunatic. I don't make any sense. I see I must take you back. A long way back, to long before you were born. Back when we were young, Flo and I."

CHAPTER 18

*H*er stitches slowed now as she began to talk of the past. "We were neither of us anything to look at, even when we were young. I think it's one of the reasons Mother and Father worked so hard to make a go of the business, so we'd always have a livelihood."

"They brought the two of us into the tea shop very early. It was always understood that we would take over Elderflower. We came of age in the 1960s. The swinging 60s. It was the time of the Beatles and, for the first time since the war, England was beginning to get back on its feet.

"London was exciting again, and people were full of hope. There was more money about. Rationing was over. Girls wore short skirts and danced in clubs until all hours. But Flo and I weren't in London. I'm not sure we'd have done any better if we were. We were a couple of plain, plump girls living in Oxford and working in an old fash-ioned tea shop. The swinging 60s virtually passed us by. However, people were beginning to have a little more money to spend, and very often they would come and spend it in the tea shop."

I felt as though she were looking back into the past and I remained quiet, fascinated to see the Oxford of her youth.

"You might think that being in Oxford, we'd be surrounded by eligible young men at the colleges, and we were. We just never really took, Flo and I." She sounded remarkably matter-of-fact about their lack of a love life, though I wondered how much of her pragmatism had come with age.

She laughed softly. "We were the sort of girls to whom young men turned for advice about their girl problems. We were like their plain cousin. I think Flo minded more than I. She was always more romantic. Perhaps she'd have left and tried for a different life given the chance. But Mother died."

Her hands stilled and she paused for a sip of tea. "She caught a bad cold. It was winter, but she wouldn't rest. We had the business to run, after all. The cold turned into pneumonia and she went quite quickly. Father was never the same after that. Flo and I took over more and more of the responsibility and he seemed to fade away. Neither of us were really surprised when he, too, passed not a year later." She smiled, sadly. "We've always said he died of a broken heart."

"They must have loved each other very much."

"Yes. We were a very happy family. We'd really never thought too much about money. We had the tea shop, of course, and we knew that Father had bought the building. But he'd also been investing, surprisingly well. We weren't wildly wealthy, but we were very comfortably set.

"We carried on, of course, because we knew that's what our mother and father would have wanted. And it was all we knew." She seemed to smile at the past. "The world is always changing, Lucy, but a good cup of tea and a decent scone doesn't. The best part of Oxford doesn't."

"I've always felt that way about Harrington Street. It changes, but not too much."

She nodded. "Well, one day, Flo came back late from doing the shopping. She was absolutely glowing. She'd met someone. It was Gerald, of course. He met her by chance it seemed. Though I don't believe that for an instant."

What did she think Gerald Pettigrew was, a stalker of plain well-to-do women? How would he even have known? I suspected jealousy at work though I still remained silent.

"Oh she was thrilled, and so happy. She said it was like something out of a film the way he'd walked smack up to her and said how heavy her bags looked and could he help carry them? Next thing I knew, they were off punting on the river and going on picnics and to the pictures. He had a car, which was much more exciting in those days than it is now, and he took her on drives around the countryside."

She put her knitting down and swiveled toward me, her hands on her hips. "And who do you think was running Elderflower?" She poked herself in the chest. "Poor old Muggins, that's who. I had to hire daily help to manage. Flo was so infatuated she couldn't see straight and she certainly couldn't think straight."

Our eyes met and she smiled ruefully. "You probably think I was jealous. I suppose I was, a little. I also admit to a certain sadness that I would be losing my sister and my best friend. I could see it happening already, but I genuinely tried to be happy for her."

"When I asked about his job and prospects she was a bit

vague. He was in sales. Motorcar sales. When I tried to pry deeper into his affairs she became annoyed with me and told me it was none of my business."

That didn't sound good, and I said so.

"It wasn't. I suppose it was none of my business, but I am the eldest and with Mother and Father gone I felt some responsibility. Also, she's my sister and I love her. I wanted to approve her choice.

"I suggested she bring him home for dinner on a Monday night. That's the only day we can entertain guests. Well, he came and he put himself out to charm me. But I saw through him right away. He was one of those people who was all charm and no substance. I suspect flattery may be his greatest talent."

"He looks as though he might be good at sales?" I ventured.

She snorted. "Selling himself to gullible women. Oh, yes. He's very good at that. When I asked him a few questions about his automotive business he chuckled and made comments suggesting that as a woman I wouldn't be able to understand. I found him patronizing and also evasive."

I had a grim picture of a very uncomfortable dinner party.

"After he left, of course Flo asked me what I thought of him. I suppose I made a grave mistake. I warned her most earnestly to find out more about him before she committed herself." She shook her head. "I didn't take into account how badly she was smitten. She must've told him what I'd said, for the next thing I knew she stopped telling me of their plans. She'd make comments about how controlling I was. I was certain they had come from him and his mission was to separate her from me."

"Oh, that must have been awful." I'd never had a brother or sister and always wished for one.

"It was," she agreed. "Then, he asked her to marry him, when they'd only known each other a few weeks. She was over the moon. Fell into his hands like the pigeon she was, ripe for the plucking. I asked her what was to happen with Elderflower? She did look sheepish, then. Said she wanted us to sell up so that she could have her half of everything." She bit her lip. "That is the only time we have ever had a genuine shouting match. We both said things that we probably regret to this day."

I suddenly pictured the two of them lobbing day old scones at each other like missiles.

"But I wasn't jealous and greedy, I was terrified for her."

"That must have been awful," I said. As an outsider, I could see both sides. I sympathized with the romantic Flo in love for the first and only time, and yet, I also sympathized with her remaining spinster sister.

"I was beside myself. When I asked her what she and Gerald proposed to do with the quite substantial amount of money she would get, she said they were planning to travel, to see the world and then they'd settle down in Australia or Canada." The outrage from all those years ago was fresh as she stared at me. "He wasn't even going to let her stay in the same country."

"And you'd have lost the shop and your livelihood."

She nodded agreement. "I may have led a sheltered life, but I'm not a fool. I foresaw nothing but heartbreak and ruin for my poor sister."

"And yet, they did not marry," I said softly. She'd been rattling the needles together as she knitted one rapid row after another. The way she was going she would have a seven-teen-foot long scarf completed before we finished our tea. "No. She didn't. Perhaps it was underhanded of me, but I hired a private investigator."

I was well and truly intrigued. Also pretty sure Mary Watt was an awesome big sister. "What did you find out?"

She looked triumphant. "He was already married."

I don't know what I'd expected, but it wasn't that. "You mean he was in the process of getting divorced?" I knew divorce was a bigger deal then, but unless you were in the Royal Family or very religious, was it enough to break up a couple in love?

"Ha! He had no intention of getting divorced. My investigator followed him to Leeds. He was living with a woman who had inherited the house they lived in and a private income. They had two children. The woman was perfectly happy, except for the fact that her husband was so often away on business."

"He was planning to be a bigamist?" I'd heard stories like this, read them in newspapers, but never actually knew anyone with two spouses. The idea was incredible.

"Yes."

"So you told your sister?"

She put her head in her hands, nearly stabbing herself in the head with her knitting needles. "I am such a fool. By that time, my sister and I were barely speaking to each other. To be honest with you, I don't think she was rational. She wouldn't have accepted the truth, even if it was given to her. I asked at one point, 'What if you found out something terrible about him?' And Flo's answer was, "There's nothing you could tell me about Gerald that would make me love him less."

"Wow. She really had it bad."

"He was such a smooth talker, you see. He could make her believe anything. And what if she went away with him and I never saw her again? I couldn't bear it. I did what I thought was the kindest thing for my poor sister." Her head was still in her hands and now she shook it vigorously. "I'm not sure I was rational at the time, either. He'd gone back to London, supposedly, and his job. But I knew where he really was."

This story was better than a TV show.

"I took out quite a large sum of money. And I drove up with the private investigator to Leeds. We confronted him together. Not at his house. Though perhaps we should have. We followed him, and, as he was about to go into a pub, I accosted him."

I could picture the scene. "He must have been stunned."

"Not that one. He's as sly as the devil. He tried to brazen it out. We went into a quiet café, the private investigator laid out his findings. Gerald claimed he hadn't been able to break the news to his missus, but he was going to ask her for a divorce so he could marry my sister, the love of his life. It was nauseating. However, he hadn't done anything illegal, yet. In hindsight I should have waited until he'd married Flo, while still married to the woman in Leeds. But how could I let Flo be humiliated that way?"

"I made Gerald Pettigrew a bargain. I told him I would give him money if he would leave Florence. I didn't care what he said to her; he could make up any story he liked, a dying mother in another country, a secret assignment from the government. He was very good at making up stories, I was sure he could invent one that would satisfy her."

"You paid him off?" I asked, sounding as astonished as I felt.

"I believed I was doing it for the best. I told him that he could take the money and go. But if I ever saw him again, I would tell Flo the whole story. Furthermore, the investigator had found out some rather unsavory facts about his past that I thought the police might quite like to know."

She looked very satisfied at that last bit.

"His phony charm dropped off his face like the mask on a street player. I truly believe that if the private investigator hadn't been there, and we hadn't been in a public place, he might have done me a violence. He agreed, in the end. He really had no choice."

Full marks to Miss Mary Watt.

"He told my sister he'd been called away. I'm not quite sure what pretext he used. He made it sound that it was his duty, and his heart was broken as hers was. It was nauseating, but at least he left Flo her dignity.

"Over time, my sister and I mended our fences. And we continued to run the shop together. During all these years, no other man has ever come between us." She laughed softly. "No other man has tried."

"And now Gerald Pettigrew is back. How could he have the gall?"

"Because I was a fool and he knew it. His wife is dead, you see. She was a fair bit older than he. Now that she's gone, he really is free. I can't tell Flo now that I separated them. You'll think me sentimental, but the older one gets, the more relationships matter. Flo is all my family and my best friend."

I thought that a woman who had sufficient gumption to hire a private detective and frighten away a fortune hunter wouldn't let the same fortune hunter steal her sister a second time. "What do you intend to do?"

"I honestly don't know. Of course, he's got my measure now. He never would have come back here if he didn't know that he has nothing to hide. Naturally, I immediately went on the internet and searched. His wife is dead. Has been for seven years."

My attentiveness was caught at that. "Seven years? Why did he take so long to come here?"

She picked up her knitting again and began winding the wool around the needle as though it were a rope around Gerald Pettigrew's neck. "I don't know. Perhaps he thought his wife would leave him enough money that he wouldn't need to defraud my poor Flo. Perhaps he tried and failed with a few other rich spinsters and widows. Maybe he's run through all the money."

"I wonder if it's worth hiring another investigator? A man who will be a bigamist once, might do it again."

She let out a sigh. "Lucy, I am eighty-two years old. Flo is eighty. I am too tired to fight this man again. If she's too foolish to realize that man is a fortune-hunting liar, then perhaps I should let her enjoy her happiness. Even if he steals all her money and leaves her, I'll still have enough left to support the two of us."

"It just seems so wrong that he should profit by seducing naïve women."

"He's not the first, and he won't be the last."

I'd been thinking. "What if he were offered a richer prize?"

She turned her head and looked at me in a puzzled fashion. "Richer prize?"

I was thinking aloud. "Colonel Montague's wife is, according to local gossip, a very wealthy widow. If the colonel was planning to divorce her, she can't be inconsolable. Maybe a much richer widow, and one who doesn't need to sell a business and properties in order to come into her money, would be more palatable to Mr. Pettigrew."

"But, Lucy, it's possible that Mrs. Montague murdered her husband. Would you want to push even a man as despicable as Gerald Pettigrew into the arms of poisoner?"

"I'd say Gerald Pettigrew is well able to look after himself. Besides, there is such a thing is divine retribution."

Mary Watt seemed much more cheerful when she left. I had taken an extra long lunch hour, but when we reached the shop Katie seemed calm and the shop running smoothly. She was, at that moment, ringing up a large order.

Miss Watt greeted her perfectly cheerfully and said she was pleased she'd found another job. Katie thanked her and said she hoped Elderflower could open again soon.

I walked Miss Watt to the door and even outside it. It was nice to take a few breaths of fresh air. She said, "I have to say that girl is a damn sight better working in your business than she was in mine."

"At the risk of sounding crass and hard-hearted, I have to say that your loss is my gain."

Miss Watt laughed. It was good to hear the sound. I suspect it had been a while since she had laughed and, the way things were going, it might be some time before she had another opportunity. She put a hand on my arm. "Thank you, Lucy. You've done me a great deal of good. I hope your grandmother's looking down on you, now. She'd be so proud."

In fact, my grandmother was hopefully sleeping peacefully, and if not, I'd put another spell on the trap door to keep her away from me. At least during store hours.

I couldn't wait to share the whole story of Gerald Pettigrew and Florence. My grandmother was an excellent judge of character. I was very curious to see what she had made of him.

I had reached the door, when a man called my name. I turned to see Ian Chisholm walking towards me. Miss Watt had also turned to look and he said, "I'm very glad to see both of you. Miss Watt, I've a few more questions I'd like to ask you."

Whatever relaxation her visit with me had achieved, was gone in an instant. Her face resumed the tight, anxious look. But she said, "Of course. Would you like to come in?"

"I would. I also have a few more questions for your waitress, Katie. Any idea where I might find her? I tried round their flat but neither she nor Jim were at home."

I said, "Katie is right behind us in the shop. She's working as my assistant."

If he was surprised at the news he hid it well. "I see." He glanced at his watch. "Miss Watt, if you've got some time now, perhaps we can talk? And then I'll come round to you, Lucy, when you close at five."

I went back into the shop and then was sorry that I hadn't asked him if it was all right to tell Katie of the treat in store for her. I thought I'd wait until nearly closing time. There was no point worrying her unnecessarily.

As the afternoon wore on I was heartily glad I had an

assistant. The amount of extra business that the murder in the tea shop had caused was amazing. We both became quite adept at tossing out platitudes about oh yes, it was a terrible shock. And no, I don't believe the police have caught the perpetrator yet. And then deftly turning the subject to knitting.

At about four forty-five, I found myself momentarily alone with Katie. The shop had emptied and I doubted we'd have any more customers before five. I said, "I bumped into Detective Inspector Chisholm earlier. He's coming here as soon as we close to ask you a few more questions. It was nice that he didn't come in during our business hours to conduct police business."

"Too right," she said. And she rubbed her arms as though she were either very cold, or very itchy, though I suspected she was just very nervous. "Any idea what he wants?"

I shook my head. "He said he had a few more questions, that's all."

"But I've told him everything I know. God, I wish I'd never come to this terrible country. It's freezing cold for a start. And everybody has a stick up their arse." In spite of the way she was insulting the very people who were paying both our salaries, her voice wavered as though she were near tears so I forgave her rudeness.

"I'm sure it's just routine," I said as soothingly as I could.

She looked at me, her eyes wide with appeal. "You won't leave me alone with him?"

I was surprised. "I was planning to go upstairs and let you have some privacy. Or, you could take him upstairs, and I can stay down the shop."

She shook her head and said no at the same time. A

double negative if ever there was one. "I want you to stay with me. Promise?"

"If the inspector allows me to, then, of course."

Ian arrived just after five with a brisk rap on the front door. I let him in and noticed he wasn't alone. He had a young constable with him. A woman about my own age. He greeted both of us and said, "Katie, I won't take up much of your time, but I've got a few more questions for you."

She said, "I don't know what I haven't told you already. And I want Lucy with me."

"Yes, that's fine."

I took them all upstairs and we settled ourselves in the living room. I quickly texted Rafe to tell him not to let my grandmother come wandering up here, which she sometimes did when the store was closed. She'd refused repeated offers for her own phone. She said she hadn't needed one in life and she certainly wasn't going to succumb to a mobile phone in death. "There are very few advantages to being undead, Lucy, but not being forced to use modern technology must count as one of them."

So, I had to rely on Rafe to get my messages to her.

The young constable drew out a notebook and Ian said, "We have the results of the post mortem."

Katie looked puzzled. "But wasn't he poisoned?"

"There was always the possibility that he died of natural causes but, as it happens, you're right. The colonel was poisoned. However, there are many substances that can poison a person and depending on the poison in the dose, we're able to accurately pinpoint when it was administered. In this case, the poison was Cyanide. It was found in his tea.

From the time he drank the tea until death would've been approximately twenty minutes."

I made the obvious inference. "So, he was definitely poisoned in the tea shop."

"He was. So, Katie, either you put the poison into the tea or you must have seen who did."

I had never seen him sound so cold and implacable before. I could feel my own heart beating harder and I wasn't the one being accused of anything. Katie went bright red and then deathly pale. She leaned forward and clasped her hands together. "I didn't kill him. Why would I? I didn't even know him. He was bloody rude, but I wouldn't kill him for that. Anyway, where would I get poison?"

"That's an excellent question. Where would you?"

"I don't know. And I didn't. That's the point."

"And yet, the tea you served the colonel is what killed him. So why don't you walk me through the exact process."

She shrank back against the sofa cushions now, and her face took on the surly look I'd become accustomed to when she worked in the tea shop. She'd been so sunny and efficient working for me that I had forgotten her much less likable side. "I already told you. I didn't make the tea that day. It was too busy. I just brought it in on the tray."

"Who prepared that tea?"

She saw the trap he was laying for her and refused to step into it. "All I know is, I didn't make the tea."

"Come on. You must know who did? There are two possibilities. Jim or Miss Watt. Which of them was it?"

She looked down at the floor. In a barely audible tone she said, "It was Miss Watt. Mary Watt."

I was startled, as I'd imagined it was Jim he was after. I

glanced at Ian's face but it gave nothing away. I knew him quite well though and I think he already knew who'd prepared that tea. Miss Watt must have told him she'd made it and Katie was only confirming what he already knew.

"And how did you know to take that particular tray to Colonel Montague's table?"

"Miss Watt told me what table number."

"You'd already given him the wrong tea once."

"Yes, I know. You don't need to keep going on about it. It was confusing and I was new. But I got it right that time."

"Who, besides you, or Miss Watt or Jim had access to that tea?"

"The tea sits there waiting to be picked up. Anyone could've gotten to it. That's what I told you before."

"Did you see anyone? It's very important you try and remember everything."

She closed her eyes. "The colonel's wife," she said. "I forgot to tell you that before. She came up, all red in the face, because he was shouting. She said something like, "For good-ness sake hurry up with the colonel's tea. He's making a scene." She looked so embarrassed."

"Did you really see that? Or are you making it up to take suspicion off you and your boyfriend?"

She was belligerent again. "No. I really did see her."

I nodded. "I saw the colonel's wife, too. She walked past our table but I thought she was headed for the bathroom. She could have been on the way to hurry his tea. I didn't watch her once she'd passed."

"Who else could have touched the tea?"

"Anyone who went to the toilet. Anyway, why couldn't someone drop the poison into the pot once it was already sitting on the table? There was that old lady fussing all over him. And I was busy running back and forth with food and cups of tea, but people were being seated, getting up and leaving, and nearly all of them had to pass by the colonel's table. Any one of them could've poisoned him."

She glanced at her watch. "Look, I'm late now. I told Jim I'd meet him after his rehearsal. We're going to see a play."

Ian said, "All right. The constable here will drive you. If you remember anything else, anything at all, you make sure and let me know." He looked at her sternly. "Just make sure it's the truth."

"Blimey. You're a charmer aren't you?" And then she grabbed her bag and said to me, "See you tomorrow?" She put a question mark on the end as Australians so often do, but in this case I really thought perhaps she was wondering if I might have reconsidered the job offer now she'd been questioned a second time by the police.

She seemed exactly as guilty today as she had on the day of the murder. Not more and not less. "Yes. Thank you, Katie. See you tomorrow."

Katie and the constable left but Ian didn't. His blue eyes were steady on my face. "I was a bit surprised to find you had hired her. You do realize she's one of the top suspects?"

Was he worried for my safety? Or did he just think I was a fool to have hired someone who could turn out to be deadly? The latter, I suspected.

"But why would she kill Colonel Montague? Why would Jim, for that matter. Have you found any connection at all between them?"

He shook his head. "No. It's got me stumped, I don't mind

telling you. Did you really see the Elspeth Montague go back toward the kitchen?"

"Oh yes. I did. I don't think I'd remembered it until Katie mentioned it. She looked a nervous wreck. He really was a most unpleasant man."

"That's what everyone says, but no one had a specific reason to kill him."

"Did the Irish woman come to see you?"

He nodded. "I think that was your doing. She seemed very anxious to make sure you weren't in any trouble."

"I think she's a decent person, though she certainly had a grudge against Colonel Montague."

"As did nearly everyone in that tea shop."

"Did she tell you why she was there?"

He settled back on the sofa and loosened his tie, as though he felt relaxed around me. It was also a subtle gesture that he was off the clock. "She did. It seems she spoke to Elspeth Montague and, although she was shocked, she seems not to have been surprised. She's promised to do the right thing by his daughter and the woman he abandoned."

"I'm glad. In all this ugliness, there are people who are acting with kindness."

His eyes twinkled with amusement. "You do like to believe the best in people, don't you?"

"What's wrong with that? I'd rather think people are good than always be suspicious of their motives."

"Good thing you run a knitting shop then, and aren't a detective."

I liked to think I was, in fact, a bit of a detective, but I also liked his assessment of me. I'd rather think the best of people than always assume the worst. But that didn't solve murders.

I told him the gossip I had heard, that the colonel had planned to divorce his wife and marry Miss Everly. "That's two December-December romances that were taking place in that tea shop. And at adjoining tables, too."

"Yes, and that's the other thing, with Katie mucking up the orders all over the place, we're not even convinced Colonel Montague was the actual target."

"The other person who'd ordered Earl Grey tea, that was on the same tray, of course, was Gerald Pettigrew." I wasn't about to break confidence with Miss Watt by telling Ian what she had told me today, but I thought a gentle hint might help his complicated investigation. I looked down at my hands. "Have you looked into Gerald Pettigrew at all?"

Ian was many things, but he was not stupid. He looked at me with that sharp blue gaze. "Why?"

"I don't know, exactly. He appeared out of nowhere, seems to have swept Florence Watt off her feet. But doesn't he seem a little too good to be true? I thought, when he first came in the shop, as he was on his way next door, that he looked like an actor. The sort who plays the retired colonel, or the aging aristocrat, on television."

He nodded. "But then, of course, those types tend to be based on real characters. He could be one. Still, we've contacted Interpol. He was last living in Australia."

My eyes widened. "Australia?"

"Yes. And he and Katie and Jim both arrived in this neighborhood within days of each other. Coincidence?"

"Well, there are nearly twenty-five million people in Australia. And the way they travel, at any time there must be thousands of them touring England, working in the shops or pubs."

He caught my gaze. "It was kind of you to give Katie a job. But you will be careful?"

I felt for the moment that he wasn't looking at me the way a cop looks at a woman who witnessed a murder. He was looking at me the way a man looks at a woman he's interested in. I felt warm and a little flustered. "I'll be careful."

His gaze was on my face. He said, "I wonder—" His phone rang at that moment. He glanced at the screen and said, "I'd better go outside and take this call. Goodbye, Lucy."

And wasn't that an ill-timed phone call? What would the rest of that sentence have been if he'd completed it? 'I wonder if you'd like to have a drink with me at the pub, Lucy? I wonder if I could interest you in dinner, Lucy? Just the two of us? I wonder if you'd like to marry me and spend the rest of your life hiding the fact that you're a witch and your grandmother is a vampire, Lucy."

I wondered why I was bothering to indulge in this pointless mental exercise.

CHAPTER 19

*I*t's funny how quickly you find a new normal after a disaster. I would have believed, once, that living and working next to the site of a murder would leave me sleepless and terrified. While I certainly made extra certain that the doors were locked and my phone was near to hand when I went to bed, I slept fine. Customers still came and went and, after the first few days, they were more interested in knitting supplies than in discussing the tragedy.

If anything, the murder was a benefit to me, since I had inherited Katie and she was the best assistant I could imagine. I liked that she was close to my age and, after the first couple of days when she was a little stiff with me, she soon opened up.

She told me about her life back in Australia. It hadn't been easy. She'd been brought up by her grandmother, not because her parents were busy professionals, as mine were, but because her mother had never left home. She'd done what menial work she could get while her own mother raised

Katie. She never mentioned her father and I wondered if she even knew who he was.

It was something she and Jim had in common, she confided in me as we tidied up the shop. His father walked out on them when he was young and his mother never recovered. "From the first time we met, we understood each other. Jim says people with happy childhoods make crap actors." She shrugged. "I think I'd rather be happy than a great actor."

"Is he enjoying his play?" I didn't know what else to say. Maybe I didn't have the most involved parents, since they were so often away on digs, but I'd always known they loved me, and visiting Gran for long stretches had always been a treat.

"He's loving it. He's playing Jack Worthing, you know, Importance of being Earnest? He came home in full makeup yesterday, just for a laugh. He did scare me, seeing this man in fancy dress at the door of the flat. He looked a completely different person. I was frightened for a moment, until I realized it was him."

Mary Watt, having used up all of the wool scraps in Gran's basket came in for more to complete a scarf that was surprisingly pretty considering the angst that had gone into its creation. She also bought wool and the pattern to make a thick, woolly jumper. "Though I don't know who I'm knitting it for. I find jumpers much too hot." So I told her about the charity effort we ran through the shop. Anyone could bring in warm sweaters for the homeless, though I had an idea that we might turn out some brand new items for a Christmas drive for the poor.

I couldn't take credit for that last idea. It was Silence Buggins who'd suggested it at Tuesday's knitting club. Back in

Victorian times, she'd been involved in a similar effort. I think she wanted to offer something useful, as her visit to the doctor who'd treated Colonel Montague had not been a success.

She and Alfred had gone together on the pretext that Silence was working on a book about early female doctors in Oxford. The meeting went well until Silence moved the subject to the recent poisoning and then the doctor had clammed up. Soon after, she'd said she had an appointment and had shown them out of her office.

"So, we don't know anything," Silence said, disheartened.

"We know that she's a feminist," Alfred had offered.

"Well, that should solve the murder," said Hester, always one to throw a damper on already dampened spirits.

Then the meeting had moved on to a discussion of Christmas in the store. Gran told me what to order plenty of and reminded me to find a teacher who could give a work-shop in knitted and crocheted Christmas ornaments. And Silence had suggested the charity knitting project.

When she heard about it, Mary Watt brightened up. She seemed to be one of those people who had a difficult time indulging herself, but if she could use her talents for others, she wouldn't feel she was wasting her time knitting.

Florence Watt and Gerald Pettigrew never came into the shop but I often saw them walking past. Usually, they were holding hands and so engrossed in each other that, if I hadn't been worried about her, I'd have found the relationship charming. But I was worried. Mary Watt did not strike me as a fanciful or particularly jealous woman. If she believed her sister was being taken advantage of, I was inclined to think she might be right.

I didn't think Gerald had moved in next door. Mary would never put up with that. But he and Florence were clearly inseparable.

Perhaps that's why I noticed so particularly when he walked by the window that Thursday morning. The bells peeled out to announce that it was noon. I still loved the bells that chimed the hour in Oxford. Rafe said those same bells had been ringing for centuries in the old churches. I happened to glance out and saw Gerald Pettigrew on his own, which was unusual. He had a distinctive stride, very military, and he was wearing a tweed jacket, gray flannels and black shoes. He always dressed smartly. On his head was a checked hat. He had a book under his arm. Hardback, and I wondered idly if he was coming or going from the public library.

Katie came up behind me and said, "Funny to see him without Miss Watt. They're always together."

I daren't hope they'd fallen out. He looked too cheerful for that.

About four o'clock that afternoon I popped out to take a deposit up to the bank. I had just passed the tea shop with the temporary sign that said closed until further notice when I heard a scream. It was a terrible scream, the kind that sends every hair on the back of your neck to full attention. It was coming from inside the tea shop. I wondered what new disaster had befallen the poor Miss Watts and went running to see what I could do to help.

The tea shop itself was dark and empty but there was light coming from the kitchen, where I could hear movement and sobbing. I walked toward the sound of heartbreak. Inside the kitchen everything was much too tidy for a restaurant kitchen. It was clear nothing had been cooked there for some days. They had a small industrial fridge, the kind you walk into. Florence Watt was on her knees in front of the open fridge. Mary Watt had her arms around her waist and was physically attempting to pull her backwards.

When she saw me she said, "Thank God. Lucy, call the police."

With the bulk of the two women in front of the fridge I had to crane my neck to see inside and I rather wished I hadn't.

It was Gerald Pettigrew. He was slumped over. Very dead. I thought he'd been strangled.

My hands trembled as I pulled out my phone. I called 999 immediately and reported the murder.

Then I went to join Mary in attempting to prevent her sister from throwing herself over Gerald and ruining any forensic evidence there might be.

We succeeded in dragging her back. The woman who had looked so young, so full of life, now looked haggard and old. The dyed blonde hair incredibly false on that collapsed face like a Christmas star still twinkling atop a long dead Christmas tree.

She turned to her sister and pointed a shaking finger. "You hated him. And you hated me to be happy. How could you? You did this."

Mary grew pale and took a step back. "Oh. Florence, I would never—how could you think it?"

But Florence Watt was beyond thinking. She began to rant at her sister, unloading all her grief and shock in a torrent of complaints and abuse. Mary tried a couple of times to defend herself and then just gave up and stood, silent, as the words poured out. I felt so helpless, standing there, and, I must admit, in the back of my mind I wondered if Florence was right. Mary had hated Gerald Pettigrew and, I believed with good cause. But would she kill him?

Of course, she was the only person who'd been on the premises for both murders, well, apart from her sister and I was fairly certain she hadn't murdered the love of her life.

The possibility had always been there that the intended victim of the poisoning was not Colonel Montague, but someone else. The pots of Earl Grey tea could easily have been mixed up by Katie. And, perhaps, Mary had decided that when she made a second attempt there would be no possibility of error.

I was tempted to get Florence a glass of water, anything to stop her mouth for a few moments and maybe give her a second to calm down, but we were standing at the scene of a murder and I didn't dare contaminate the area further.

"Why don't we move out of the kitchen and wait for the police in the tea shop?"

Florence didn't stop ranting long enough to hear my words and Mary seemed too stunned to react. I said, again, louder this time, "Florence. Mary. Let's go into the tea shop and wait for the police there."

Florence looked at me aghast. "I can't leave Gerald. Look how cold he is. I can't leave him there." And then she began to sob, long, ragged heartbroken sobs. Perhaps she'd get as much relief in tears as she had in words she could never take back.

She was bent over like a broken doll and Mary and I were able to each put an arm around her and walk her out of that terrible kitchen and back to the tea shop. I found some bottled water and gave each of the women a bottle and we settled to wait. It wasn't very long before the portly chief detective inspector and Ian had returned and with them was the young constable who'd come with Ian to interview Katie, and two more police officers in uniform. It was me who let them in, both Mary and Florence remaining unmoving when the doorbell chimed.

If they were surprised to see me, no one showed it. The portly detective said, "Was it you who phoned in the murder?"

"Yes, it was." I gave him my name and the fact that I lived next door in case they might've forgotten and then I let them into the tea shop. The chief inspector motioned with his head for Ian to go into the kitchen and he sat at the table with the two ladies. I'm not sure Florence even noticed someone new had joined them. Her tears were flowing so fast and thickly I don't think she could see. Between her hiccuping sobs and disjointed phrases of accusation, I doubted she could hear anything, either.

All this he took in. Mary's face as pale as a marble effigy and her sister, who had enough animation for the two of them, crying and wailing, rocking herself back and forth. After a minute or two he said gently, but quite firmly, "Miss Watt, I am very sorry that you've suffered another tragedy in such a short time, but I must ask you to tell me what happened."

He was clearly speaking to Florence Watt and so Mary looked at him for a moment and then back to her sister. Finally, Florence pulled a cotton handkerchief out of the sleeve of her sweater and mopped her eyes and nose. "We were going to the pictures. At that nice old theater on Walton Street that shows the classics and art house movies. We were going to see Lawrence of Arabia, because I'd never seen it and Gerald told me how much I'd enjoy it."

She wiped away her tears with her hanky. "But he was late. And he's never late."

"What time was this?" The inspector asked her.

"He was to pick me up at three as the film started at four. By three-thirty I was worried and I came down to see if he was out on the street. I looked up and down and I didn't see him and so I came back in and then I saw that the light was on in the kitchen. Of course, we're closed, I couldn't understand why anyone would be in the kitchen. I thought perhaps Gerald had gone into the kitchen. It didn't make any sense. I wasn't thinking very clearly because I went into the kitchen. There was no one there. I called out, I don't know why, because the kitchen was empty. Of course, there was no answer. And then I saw the fridge door was ajar."

She buried her head in her hands. And it was a moment before she could speak. Mary tried to rub her shoulder, but her sister shrugged her off. When she spoke again, she said, "I tried to shut the door but something was in the way. And then I opened it and looked in." Once again her voice was suspended by tears and she had to swallow before she could finish, "And there he was."

"Gerald Pettigrew?"

"Yes."

"Did you touch him or try to revive him at all?"

"No. I could tell he was dead. I think I screamed. Because the next thing I knew, Mary was there. And then, and then Lucy from next door. Not sure why she was there."

He glanced to me as though thinking it was a fair question. I said, "I heard Florence scream from out on the street."

"And who let you in?"

"The front door was ajar. I suppose that's why I was able to hear the screams so clearly. I knocked on the open door and walked in and heard the commotion." I looked at Mary. "I thought someone was hurt."

She smiled, a pale semblance of her normal warmth. "I'm glad you did come in."

She said to the inspector, "Lucy had the sense to get us all out of the kitchen as quickly as possible."

"And did you touch anything, Miss Swift?"

So hard to remember in retrospect. Had I? "I may have touched the door leading into the kitchen, I don't remember. Other than that I only touched Mary and Florence."

"Did you see the deceased?"

I had to swallow before I could speak and it was an effort to repress a shudder. "Yes. Yes I did."

"And you would confirm Miss Watt's assertion that he was already dead?"

"Oh yes." I didn't want describe the scene. He could take a look himself.

He looked me again. "You say the door was open, the door to the street?"

"Yes, I suppose I didn't think too much of it because normally the door always is open. That is when the tea shop is in business."

He looked to the two Miss Watts. "How long has that door been unlocked?"

Mary Watt said, "As far as I knew it had remained locked since," her voice wobbled, "the last murder."

Florence said, "It was me, I think. When I went out to the street to look for Gerald."

"And you're certain it was locked when you went to look for Mr. Gerald Pettigrew at approximately three-thirty?"

She looked like a college student terrified she was about to fail a final. "I think so. But now, I'm not sure."

He looked at her steadily for a moment but she didn't have anything more to add. He asked, "Who else has been in the house, today?"

Mary answered, "Only Elspeth Montague. She's a friend of mine."

Ian returned and said, "You'll want to take a look, sir." The chief inspector nodded and rose. He and Ian both went back into the kitchen. They were gone a surprisingly short time and then they returned together. He told one of the constables to stand outside and wait for the forensics team and the police photographer.

Then he asked, "You're certain that is Gerald Pettigrew?"

Florence nodded and then said in a voice that was barely a whisper, "Yes."

"And when did you last see him, Miss Watt?"

"See him? Alive? Last night. We had dinner out. At that nice restaurant on top of the Ashmolean. He said it made him feel less old to dine above the mummies." And she burst into tears.

"And what time did he leave you?"

"About eleven. He walked me home. Even though it's not far, he's very old-fashioned that way and has such good manners. Had, I mean. I invited him in but, well Mary didn't like him very much, so he refused." She began to cry again. "Perhaps if he'd come in with me, he'd still be alive."

He turned to Mary Watt. "And when did you last see Mr. Pettigrew?"

Her gaze dropped to her hands, which I noticed were restless suddenly in her lap. For some reason I was reminded of the manic knitting. She said, "I saw them coming home last night, from the upstairs window. It was about eleven."

"So, no one's seen him since eleven o'clock last night?"

"I have," I said. And suddenly all gazes turned to me. I reported seeing Gerald Pettigrew earlier that day.

"And what time was that?"

I thought back. "It was exactly noon. I heard the bells chiming."

"Did you speak to him?"

"No. I saw him across the street. I was in the shop and I suppose it seemed remarkable to see him alone. Normally when I see him he's with Miss Watt. He had a book in his hand. The light hit the jacket cover as he swung his arm, looked like a library book."

"And what was he wearing. Do you remember?"

"A checked cap, a tweed jacket. There was a scarf around his neck, I think. And he had on woolen trousers that I think were brown, no, wait, gray and black walking shoes."

"You're very observant."

"Gerald Pettigrew was always well turned out. That's why his clothing caught my attention. He looked every inch the retired gentleman." I felt a little sad as I said, "Dapper. That's the word I would have used to describe him."

"Yes," Florence said, "he was always so well-dressed. So gentlemanly." And she began to cry again. This time Mary didn't even try to soothe or touch her.

He said to one of the constables, "You. Check the local libraries, see if Gerald Pettigrew had a library card and if he took out or returned a book today."

"Yes, sir," the young woman said and left.

A SLIGHT DISTURBANCE occurred when the police photographer arrived and, close behind him, the forensics team. Two men with a stretcher came in last and it was all so familiar, I think all three of us who'd been present at the last murder felt terrible, with a sinking sense of déjà vu. I certainly did. I think it was even the same two men.

That was the last straw for poor Florence Watt. She took one look at the stretcher and the body bag and laid her head in her arms on the table. I said to the Inspector, in a low voice, "Would it be all right if I took Miss Watt next door? I think, perhaps, a doctor should be called. She's making herself ill with grief."

He nodded. "Yes. I must just ask the two ladies one more question. Could each of you tell me your movements since eleven o'clock last night?"

Mary Watt was still watching her very busy hands in her lap. She said, "Florence and I spoke briefly when she came home. Then, I went to bed. I got up this morning about seven, had my breakfast and so on, and then I went out to do some shopping."

"And what time was that?"

She shook her head. "About nine, I think, perhaps half past?" She seemed to be thinking back on her day. There was a pause. And then she said, "I stopped for coffee and came back about twelve-thirty I should think. I made some lunch and then I sat in the front room with the television on, knitting. Elspeth came by for a visit." She looked at me and said,

"Without the tea shop to run, I haven't found a routine yet. I'm so pleased I've got the knitting to do."

"And Miss Florence? I know this is difficult for you, but I must ask you to try and tell me everything you did after you left Mr. Pettigrew last night."

Her handkerchief was so wet that I dug in my handbag and found a package of tissues and pushed them across the table to her. She mopped up once more and then said, "I woke up about eight. I had my breakfast. Normally, Gerald and I would make plans to spend the whole day together but he said he had some business to attend to this morning, that's why we weren't meeting until this afternoon."

"Did he say what this business of his was?"

"Something to do with his investments, I think. I got the feeling he was going to the bank."

"Did he mention anything about a book? Or going to bookshop or library?"

"No. But he was a great reader."

"Did he say what time this appointment was?"

She shook her head. "I wish I'd thought to ask him. I never thought it would be important."

"Do you know which bank he used?"

Once more she shook her head.

"I'm sorry to ask you this, Miss Watt, but do you have any idea who his next of kin was?"

She shook her head. "Gerald didn't have any family. He had a wife who was sickly. He had to look after her, and then she died last year and he was finally free to come and find me."

I caught Mary's eye and she nodded. She was going to have to tell the police about his other family. If she was right, and the man we knew as Gerald Pettigrew had had a wife and family up in Leeds, then presumably his now adult children were his next of kin.

The chief inspector said to Florence, "You go next door with Lucy. I'll come and talk to you again, soon."

She grabbed the sleeve of his coat with her hand, her fingers curled like claws. "You'll catch who did this? You'll find them and punish them?"

He said, gently, "That's our job."

I rose and said, "Come on, Miss Watt. Let's go next door." To her sister I said, "Is there any chance your doctor makes house calls?"

"We've seen Dr. McNeil as long as he's been in practice, and his father before him. I'll make sure he comes and treats Florence. You just keep her nice and quiet at your place."

"I'll do my best. Why don't you come as well and bring your knitting?"

"In a minute. I've something to say to the chief inspector, first."

I nodded. And I helped Florence out of her chair. To my surprise, Ian, said, "I'll come next door with you ladies."

I did not think he was being chivalrous. I wondered if he wanted to interview Miss Watt away from her sister and then I realized, of course, that Katie was now working in my shop. Sure enough, when we reached the knitting shop, the closed sign was on the door but Katie, bless her, had remained. When the three of us walked in, her eyes widened in surprise at the sight of the detective and a clearly distraught Miss Watt. She said, "I didn't want to leave, in case you needed me."

"Thank you." I said, "I'm just going to take Miss Watt upstairs and make a cup of tea. Ian can fill you in."

She looked as though she wished very much that she hadn't stayed behind. She didn't seem to relish another interview with the detective. She looked at me. "What's going on? What's happened?"

He shook his head at me and said, "I'm glad you're still here. I have a few more questions for you."

As I ushered Miss Watt through the door to the stairway that led to my private quarters upstairs I heard him say, "How well did you know Gerald Pettigrew?"

"Who?"

"I made her promise never to lie to me again. She promised." These words sprang, unprompted, from Florence Watt's mouth and seemed unconnected to anything except, I imagined, her thoughts, which she had not so far shared with me.

I was quite worried about the younger Miss Watt. She'd come straight upstairs and slumped on my sofa as though her legs wouldn't hold her. Even her spine seemed compromised, as though all her bones had gone soft in the last half hour. My heart actually ached for her. Not only had her lover been murdered and she'd found the body, but I feared she was about to find out he was a bad man. I wasn't certain if discovering he was not the man she had thought he was would be a benefit to her in the days to come, but strangely I didn't think so. Florence Watt struck me as a woman who believed other people were good because she herself was so good. Gerald had certainly invented a character for her to fall in love with and she had obligingly helped him, adding further virtues to the ones he had assumed. She had already lost him once. To find he hadn't been that man at all, well, who would she grieve?

I hoped that Mary Watt would be able to convince the doctor to come and visit Florence. In the meantime, all I could do was offer her tea and an ear if she wanted it. Nyx must've heard the commotion for she came walking daintily out of my bedroom, yawning. She'd been out all night doing I know not what and had spent most of the day sleeping. Her green eyes blinked a few times and then she walked over to the couch, jumped on it, and then stepped into Miss Watt's lap.

I didn't know if Florence liked cats so I stood by for a moment in case Nyx needed removing, but Florence seemed comforted saying, "Oh what a sweet little puss," and stroking her with shaking hands. Nyx circled once and then curled up on the woman's lap, immediately beginning to purr.

I made strong English breakfast tea, what Gran called builders tea, and put lots of sugar in it. I set it before Miss Watt with a plate of biscuits and thought how strange it was that only a couple of days ago I'd been entertaining her sister in that very spot. Knitting had seemed to sooth Mary Watt and I wondered if would have the same effect on her sister. "Do you knit?" I asked her.

She looked up from cooing at the cat, and blinked at me as though reviewing my words and then making sense of them. "Oh, no. I've never been able to get on with knitting, or crochet. My mother used to tat, but I can't do that either. The only womanly art I was ever any good at was cooking. Gerald says my scones are the best in England." She glanced at me and her face creased. A single tear tracked down her cheek. "Said. I meant, Gerald said."

"I'm so sorry."

"I don't know how I'll ever get used to it. He was so alive, you see. I never knew anyone so full of life as Gerald was." She stared at me in puzzled horror. "Why would anyone do such a terrible thing?"

I noticed that she didn't say who, but why. I waited.

"We were getting married. That's why she killed him."

The line came out of nowhere and I was so shocked I asked her to repeat herself, thinking perhaps I hadn't heard correctly. She said, "It's true. We weren't going to the pictures at all today. We were going to get married, quietly, at the registry office, so Mary couldn't stop us. She saw him, this morning. And he told her. That's why she killed him."

"You mean your sister Mary?" I wanted to be absolutely certain she was accusing her sister.

"Oh yes. Such betrayal. It must have been her, it's the only thing that makes sense. I've been thinking and thinking. She must have seen him downtown this morning and he told her of our plans. Who else would want Gerald Pettigrew dead?"

I wished that Ian or another properly trained investi-gator were here with me. I felt that I must be very, very careful in how I asked questions and how I listened to the answers. This woman was gripped with terrible despair and grief and I wasn't entirely certain that it hadn't temporarily disordered her mind. "Did you speak to Gerald this morning?"

"No. He didn't want to see or speak to me until he picked me up. He said it would be bad luck." She wiped another tear away. "Oh, how I wish I'd spoken to him, one last time."

"Did Mary tell you she saw Gerald this morning?"

She stared at me like I was stupid. "She'd hardly tell me

she'd seen him this morning, if she was going to murder him, now would she?"

I tried again. "Did someone see them together and tell you?"

"No, no, nothing like that. But Mary told you herself she did the shopping this morning and then stopped for coffee. The only place we stop for coffee when we do our shopping is Pistachios on Broad Street. That's where Gerald goes, you see. Every morning when he's not with me he gets his paper and a coffee and croissant. I believe they met up with each other, no doubt a chance meeting. And Gerald, lovely man that he was, must have told her our plans and invited her to the wedding."

She took a sip of her tea and the cup rattled when she placed the cup back on the saucer. "He knew how much I wanted her to be my bridesmaid—that sounds too ridiculous at our age, but she was the person I wanted to stand up for me. But she's been so unpleasant to Gerald, we decided not to tell her, knowing she'd try and talk me out of marrying him. But I believe he met her and told her of our plans. Why else would she kill him?"

I thought for a moment. "But you two are more than sisters. You're best friends and business partners, do you really think your sister would murder the man you loved?"

She wiped at another tear. I had given her my only packet of tissues so I found some of Gran's lace edged linen napkins in a bureau drawer and put a stack of them on the table. Florence helped herself with a muttered thank you. She said, "There's a side to Mary you don't know. There's a side to Mary no one sees. Oh she's lovely and charming in the tea shop, when the customers are there, but she can be very nasty. She split us up, you know. All those years ago."

I did know, because Mary had told me, but I was very surprised that Florence knew. "Did Mary tell you that?"

She blew her nose on the napkin. "Not until I forced her to. It was Gerald who told me. He was very reluctant, but he felt it was only right I know. He didn't want to have any secrets from the woman he was going to marry."

I thought to myself he had another reason for his confession. At least, if Mary was right about him, he did. The trouble was, as I was beginning to see, the two sisters had very different versions of the events, and it wasn't easy to sort out whose was the correct one. Certainly, Gerald was dead, had been strangled, presumably in the kitchen of the tea shop, where he'd been found. Which did suggested it was an inside job. I didn't want to think of Mary as a murderer. But I was beginning to wonder if she might be one.

There were too many stories about the past. That was the trouble. All these grim, dark deeds had taken place half a century ago. Had Gerald really had another woman and another family, or had Mary made up that story to discredit him in my eyes? Perhaps even then she'd been planning to do away with him and wanted to blacken his character.

Proof. That's what was lacking here, proof. All I had was stories, old stories at that.

"What did Gerald tell you that Mary did all those years ago?"

"She threatened him with exposure. She found out, you see, about his top secret assignment and she threatened to tell the Russians."

I felt my eyes widen. "The Russians?"

She looked at me as though I were a particularly dim

student in history class. "It was the Cold War. Gerald was on a top-secret mission. He could have been killed."

"And you confronted your sister with this? Did she admit what she'd threatened?"

She gave a bitter laugh. "Of course not. She made up some story about Gerald having another woman. As if I wouldn't know if the man I loved was seeing another woman. It was pitiful. I never knew until that moment how jealous she was. Gerald kept telling me she was but I didn't believe it. I wish I had believed him. I wish I'd run away with him as he kept asking me to. But I didn't see why we should. This is my home, half of that business is mine and half the property. No. I was determined to stay and fight for what was mine." She buried her face in one of the linen napkins. "And now I've lost Gerald. The man who meant more to me than anything. I don't know how I'll go on. We had such plans, you see. We were going to travel all over the world. He wanted me to see all the places he'd been."

"That would have been wonderful. But you can still travel."

"I've hardly traveled anywhere, you see. There was always the tea shop. We were so busy. Mary and I got away a few times and had a week's holiday, but I've never seen the world. Now I suppose I never will."

She finished her tea and then lifted the cat off her lap and stood. "Well, I'd better go down and see that nice young detective. I don't relish what I have to do, but I'm afraid, if you'll excuse me, I have to turn my sister in for murder."

CHAPTER 20

I didn't know what to do. Nyx and I stared at each other for a moment. The cat seemed to be saying, "Stop her."

If Florence went to the police and accused her own sister of murder, Mary and Florence would never get their relationship back.

While I was dithering, a knock sounded on my outside door. When I went to answer it, I found Mary Watt on the other side of the door and with her a man she introduced as Dr. Finlayson. She said, "I won't come in. How is she?"

How on earth did I answer that? "She's still very upset." And left it at that.

She nodded. Then she reached out and put a hand on my arm. "I hope you didn't take any notice of all her crazy talk earlier. She didn't mean all those cruel things she was saying to me." Then she looked at me as though trying to convince both of us and said, "I'm sure she didn't."

I nodded. "Don't worry, we'll look after her."

"Thank you, dear. I must get back."

When I took the doctor into the sitting room, Florence looked surprised. "I heard a man's voice, and I thought it was that nice detective. Dr. Finlayson? What are you doing here?"

Dr. Finlayson was on the older side though he was probably two decades younger than his patient. Still, he spoke to her in a fatherly manner. "I heard about your trouble, Florence, and I'm very sorry. How are you feeling?"

"Oh, Dr. Finlayson, it's been so dreadful."

The doctor sat beside her and took her hand and, being neither relative or a member of the medical profession, I decided the best thing for me to do was to make myself scarce. Also, I was bit worried that my grandmother might not have got the message and decide to pay me a visit and the last thing poor Miss Watt needed was to be confronted by a woman she knew to be dead.

I slipped downstairs and through the connecting door into the shop. To my surprise, Katie was still there, although Ian had left. My new assistant was tidying up. She had the duster in her hand and a polishing cloth in the other. "Katie, you didn't have to stay so late."

"That's all right. I thought the shop could do with tidying and besides," she made a face. "I don't want to be home alone. Not with murderers about. Jim is rehearsing. He's been there all day, and he just called to tell me they're staying on tonight to smooth out some technical difficulties. Lighting, I think."

I fetched the broom and swept up the floor. "It's unnerving, that's for sure." I didn't know how much she'd heard about the second murder so I stuck to platitudes. In truth I was a bit nervous, too.

She paused in her dusting and was looking intently at one of the knitted pieces hanging on the wall. One Sylvia had created. "This is one of the most beautiful, and intricate, pieces of knitting I've ever seen in my life. Whoever did it must have knitted their entire life to get this good."

In fact, Sylvia had spent the better part of a century perfecting her craft. "It is beautiful, isn't it? I've discovered that displaying finished pieces really inspires our regular customers to up their game."

She and her duster moved on and so did her train of thought. Her next comment was, "It's awful about that poor old man getting killed next door. I mean the second old man."

"Terrible." I recalled now that when Ian had questioned her about Gerald Pettigrew she had looked blank.

I said, "Did you really not know Gerald Pettigrew?"

"Well, I saw him often enough, and I knew he was Miss Watt's boyfriend but I never knew his name. Friendly bloke, though, and liked to have a laugh. He had an eye to the ladies, too."

"Really? Why do you say that?"

"Oh, it was all harmless fun, but he liked to flirt. Old, young, pretty or plain, he didn't mind. He toned down a bit when either of the Miss Watts was about, but there was nothing in it. As I said, it was harmless fun."

Katie said, "DI Chisholm wanted to know if I had ever seen the old boy before coming to England. Seems he spent some time in Australia. Well, bully for him, so do lots of people. He'll have to do better than that if he wants to connect me with the old boy's murder."

"Do you think he was trying to?"

She stopped dusting and turned to look at me. I could see the troubled frown. "Seems like I'd be an easy scapegoat. Not from here, don't have a family, who'd complain if I got done for it? The local cops look like heroes and I spend the rest of my life in jail."

It was an absurd idea but I could see that she was nervous. "I'd care. You're the best assistant I've ever had. If anybody tries to arrest you they better have a damn good case. Don't worry. The police won't arrest anyone if they don't have good cause. And you're not friendless."

She looked pleased, but then her mouth turned down. "I appreciate the support but you're not exactly a pillar of the community yourself. You're only about my age and you're an outsider, too. No offense, but I'll need more friends than you if they decide to point the finger at me."

I wanted to tell her that I could call on the resources of any number of creatures who had lots of time, lots of history, and underground networks that stretched around the world. I'd back my vampire network against Interpol any day. I couldn't tell her that so I said, "Try not to worry. Hopefully they'll catch the real killer and we can all sleep at night."

"He definitely thinks I'm the prime suspect, you know. He wanted to know if we had a key for next door."

"Did you?"

She nodded, a worried frown creasing her forehead. "We went in early, you see. Jim to start baking and me to set up. But we gave it back when they closed the tea shop."

I began to see why she was feeling so nervous. Very few people would have had access to the tea shop kitchen when the entire place was closed and locked up.

But Katie had no motive.

Miss Mary Watt on the other hand had a great deal of motive. I wondered if she had told the detectives what she knew of Gerald Pettigrew's past. I hoped she had because it was the right thing to do. However, if she'd murdered him, she'd be putting a noose around her own neck. It put me in an awkward position because she had confided in me. If she hadn't told the police what she knew, did I have an obligation to tell them?

I did not relish the idea of being a snitch but neither did I relish the idea that a murderess might get away with her crime. Especially if she'd killed the colonel as well.

Did anything connect the two men? Clearly I needed to call on my network.

There was a tap on the door and we both jumped, before she peeked out the window. "It's Jim. See you tomorrow, then, if I haven't been arrested."

The back of my neck had chilled a couple of times in the last half hour so I knew that one or more vampires had attempted to come into my shop. I'd left the lock on the trapdoor. While it wouldn't stop them if they were determined to come up, they all seemed to respect that if that door was locked it wasn't safe.

Florence Watt was still upstairs but I didn't want to bother her if she was still with the doctor. Given the circumstances, I knew she wouldn't want to sleep in her own home, not when her lover had been murdered there and she suspected her own sister. Part of me wanted to offer her my spare room, but might Miss Mary Watt interpret that as me taking sides in their dispute?

I badly needed my grandmother's advice. She was always good at questions of social etiquette.

I went into my back room and quickly unlocked the trap-door and went down the stairs into the tunnel. As many times as I did this, it always took me a moment to adjust to the slightly dank air and the damp chill. Rafe had assured me there were no rats in the tunnel but I walked quickly anyway. I rapped on the door, which was opened immediately, almost as if they had been waiting for me.

It was Sylvia who opened it, looking glamorous as usual, this time in a red and silver knit dress that showed off her admirable figure. She said, "Lucy. What on earth is going on above stairs?"

I smiled at her quaint terminology. As though we were in the servants' quarters of a large country house. "It's been a hell of a day."

"Well, you'd better come in and tell us all about it. Your grandmother's been most anxious."

I nodded and entered the room. Gran was sitting in the corner at the computer and turned to look at me, with an expression of horror. "I've just been searching for news on the dark net."

Of course, vampires embraced technology, and had probably invented the dark net. If not, they certainly took advantage of its secret underground networks. "What dreadful news. Poor Miss Watt. Poor both of them. How are they taking it?"

I hadn't come in bursting with news and expecting to astonish them all, but I was slightly deflated to arrive and find they already knew about the drama. "Both the Miss Watts are taking it very hard. Do you know who the latest victim was?"

"No. That information hasn't been released, not in official circles or unofficial ones. Who was it?"

At least I could tell them that. "It was Gerald Pettigrew. The man that Miss Florence Watt was planning to marry this very afternoon."

"Oh poor, dear, Florence. I wish I could go up and tell her how sorry I am. I hope you said what was proper for both of us."

"Of course I did. In fact, I think she's still upstairs. Her doctor's with her. Dr. Finlayson."

Gran nodded. "He wouldn't be my choice of a doctor. He's a bit of a fusspot, but he suits a pair of old spinsters like the Miss Watts. He holds their hand and listens to their complaints and prescribes tonics that probably don't have any medicinal ingredients, but make them feel better."

I couldn't help but smile, as that was exactly the impression I'd had of Dr. Finlayson. "I hope he can give her something to make her feel better or at least to sleep."

There were about half a dozen vampires sitting around the main room. One was doing a crossword puzzle, one was checking her stocks on her iPad and three were knitting. Rafe wasn't among them and I knew without being told that he wasn't on the premises. I seemed to have a particular instinct about him that I didn't have about any of the others. It was a bit annoying, like an unwanted GPS that you could never turn off.

As though she had read my mind, Gran said, "Rafe's missing all the excitement. He's in Liverpool, evaluating a private collection. There is said to be a first edition of David Copperfield. Of course, Rafe calls all Dickens' work popular rubbish, but I suppose to a man who was at court when Shakespeare was penning and performing his plays, a little snobbishness is acceptable."

"I want to ask your advice, Gran."

She looked quite pleased. "Of course. Do you want to be private? Shall I send the others away?"

"No, no."

The woman on her iPad said, "What the bloody hell is going on with the euro?"

The one doing the crossword puzzle said, "I told you to stick with bitcoin. Currency trading is a mug's game."

The three knitters were talking amongst themselves. I didn't think I needed to worry about anyone overhearing us. I pushed a chair closer to the computer and explained my dilemma. How Mary had paid off Gerald Pettigrew years ago, which Florence didn't know, and how Florence believed Mary had murdered her fiancé, which Mary didn't know.

Gran listened intently to the whole story. "What a silly pair! If I was still alive I'd go over there and knock some sense into the pair of them. They've only got each other. What will happen to them if they turn on each other?"

"I agree with you. But do you think I can offer Miss Florence Watt our spare room? I feel we should keep the two sisters apart, at least for the next few days. I doubt she'll want to sleep in the same place where her lover was murdered."

My grandmother nodded. "You're very wise. Give her some time to calm down before she accuses her sister of murder."

"Exactly. I feel like if they could talk to each other they might have information between them that could help."

"Unless Mary did kill Gerald Pettigrew. In which case, I doubt the relationship could be saved."

"Does Mary seem remotely like a murderer to you?"

She made a clicking noise with her tongue against the

roof of her mouth. "No, but did I think that nice young man who killed me was a murderer? Not until he ran me through with an antique dagger."

Clearly, she was still having some issues transitioning to being undead. Not that I blamed her. "Perhaps anyone has it in them to kill, given the right provocation. My new assistant is still under suspicion."

From behind me Sylvia said, "You mean that young waitress whom you hired as your assistant?"

I hadn't heard the glamorous vampire sneak up on me. Clearly she'd heard the entire conversation so far. "Yes. Katie believes the police are trying to make a connection between her and the dead man. Based on the fact that she's Australian and he had spent some time there. She's young and friendless and has no money and she's worried that they're going to pin this on her for the sake of an easy arrest."

Sylvia said, "I don't have the greatest respect for policing today. They've become so lazy. They rely entirely too much on forensics and too little on common sense and instinct. Did she know the victim?"

"She says not."

Clearly she had heard the note of doubt in my voice. "And you think she did?"

"I'm in a terrible dilemma," I admitted. "I've known the two Miss Watts since I very first came to Oxford. They're like my own maiden aunts. So I can't bear the thought that one of the might have murdered the other's fiancé. On the other hand, Katie is my new assistant and she's very efficient. I don't want her to be a murderer, either. But who else is there?"

"What about the boyfriend? Presumably, he's as much a suspect as she is?"

"Katie said he'd been in rehearsal all day for this play he's in. He started rehearsing at twelve-thirty. Katie and I both saw Gerald Pettigrew walk by at noon. Jim couldn't possibly have murdered Gerald, put his body into the fridge of the tea shop, and got to his rehearsal on time, not within thirty minutes. That's why they like her."

"But wasn't she working with you?"

I sighed. "Yes, she was. But she took her lunch break late. We were so busy through the normal lunch rush that she didn't get away until one-thirty. She was actually a few minutes late coming back at two-thirty. She could've seen him, enticed him to take her into the kitchen on some pretext, murdered him, and still had plenty of time to eat her sandwich and return to work."

"She'd have to be a pretty cool customer."

"Yes. Also, she would have to have a motive. I want to see justice done as much as any person, but I won't let her be arrested for no other reason than that she was in the right place at the right time."

"And the doors to their home and shop were locked? All day?"

"Both Miss Watts say so. Florence opened the door at about three-thirty looking for Gerald because he hadn't turned up. That's why it was unlocked when I went in, but she swears she had to unlock it."

"Who else has keys to that place? Are there tradesmen? Friends?"

Gran and I exchanged glances. I said, "There's a key to Elderflower hanging in my kitchen."

"So that wretched girl could have snuck up when you were busy, pinched the key, done the deed, and put it back again. Always assuming, of course, that the old charmer didn't let her in without her even needing a key."

"Yes."

"Right. What do you want us to do?"

"Can you find out if Katie had any connection at all to Gerald Pettigrew? In fact, find out what you can about Mr. Pettigrew, who seems a shady character."

"Child's play. Anything else?"

"Yes. Mary claimed that she hired a private investigator fifty years ago who discovered that Gerald Pettigrew had a second family in Leeds. In fact, when he asked Florence to marry him, he was already married and a father of two. However, Florence believes that her sister got rid of Gerald by tumbling onto some secret assignment he had as a spy and threatening to expose him. It would've ruined his career and, I suppose, threatened the security of the United Kingdom."

"Heavens. What widely different stories."

I nodded. "I need to know which one is the truth."

"Any idea who this private investigator was?"

"It was so long ago, he could be dead."

Sylvia sighed. "They'll be no Internet records, of course. Do we know if Gerald Pettigrew is his real name?"

I stared at her. "No. I hadn't even thought that."

She rubbed her hands together. "I do relish a challenge. Leeds," she pulled a face. "Why couldn't he have a second family in Paris, or Prague, or someplace I'd quite like to visit? Leeds is such a dreary place. Which somehow lends credibility to the story. Never mind, I shall take a trip up there. Agnes? Would you care to join me?"

My grandmother looked both flattered and somewhat

appalled at the idea of traveling to Leeds. "Oh. I hadn't thought. Lucy, won't you need me here?"

I exchanged a quick glance with Sylvia. It would be a good thing for my grandmother to get out of town for a couple of days. She was still too concerned with her old friends among the living and it wouldn't do any of us any good if she decided to throw caution to the winds in order to comfort either or both of the Miss Watts. "I'll miss you, of course, but Gran, think of the good you could do."

"Anything to help you, my dear. And poor Mary and Florence as well. Though I don't know whether I want him to turn out to be a nasty bigamist and a cad, or a spy who gave up the woman he loved rather than compromise the safety of this nation."

A rather portly man with wispy blond hair and a face as innocent as a newborn baby's made a noise like humph. We all turned to look at him but he was engrossed in his knitting and the humph could have been an expression of irritation at his knitting rather than a comment on Gerald Pettigrew's patriotism, or lack of it.

Sylvia said, "How very strange to have two old men murdered in Elderflower Tea Shop within the same week. Is there a serial killer of old gentlemen about?"

"Katie was the most hopeless waitress and kept getting the table numbers mixed up. I believe now that Gerald Pettigrew was the intended victim all the time."

The portly blond man, with his eyes still on his knitting, said, "Never jump to conclusions. That's bad police work."

I glanced at him in surprise but he just kept knitting. Sylvia said, "Theodore was a policeman. He's very particular about proper procedures being followed."

Theodore nodded. "Don't believe in hunches. Nor in jumping to conclusions. Plodding footwork, that's what you want."

I was delighted to have a professional to discuss this case with. "But there doesn't seem to be any connection between the two gentlemen."

His eyes might be baby soft but his voice was hard as he mimicked me. "*Doesn't seem? Doesn't seem?* That's your idea of investigation is it, missy? You want to dig and dig until you can say with absolute certainty where the connection is between them, for I'll be bound there is one. The two men didn't have to know each other, they only have had to have hurt the same person or—if it is indeed a serial killer—fit some profile."

I said, "Well, we know that Colonel Montague was in the military. I've been discounting Gerald Pettigrew's Secret Service story as a tall tale told to cover up his philandering and possible bigamy. What if he actually was in the Secret Service? Could he and the colonel have worked on the same case? Perhaps someone from the past is out to get them."

He nodded, looking mildly pleased. "That's the ticket. Now, you take that question and you search. It's a theory. Can you prove it?"

"It's a wild guess," I said helplessly.

"Doesn't matter. That's how we start. And while you're following that line of inquiry you also follow the other, that Gerald Pettigrew was the intended victim all the time. Why? Who wanted to kill him so badly that he–he wagged a finger —or she would also murder an innocent victim?"

It was uncomfortable work thinking about hate and

murder. Miserably, I said, "Florence Watt believes her sister Mary may be the culprit."

Gran shook her head. "Imagine thinking so badly of the person you've been close to all your life."

Sylvia said, "Agnes, I think we should leave now. The roads will be quiet and we can begin our investigations and leads first thing in the morning."

The former policeman said, "Ladies, I shall accompany you. I feel you need a trained investigator."

Sylvia raised her fine eyebrows but merely said, "So long as you don't think you're driving. We'll take my Bentley."

Gran seemed quite excited about the adventure. "I don't think I've ever been driven in a Bentley."

Sylvia shook her head. "We're going to have a talk about compound interest. In a couple of generations you will be as rich as the rest of us."

"What, rich enough for a Bentley?"

"With your own chauffeur, should you wish one," Sylvia said grandly. "Of course, we try not to live too opulent a life-style. We take care not to draw too much attention to ourselves."

I could see that they were anxious to get going. "You will be careful, won't you?" They looked at me, puzzled, and I realized there wasn't much that could hurt them. Still, Gran was a brand new vampire. I felt she needed to be cautious.

CHAPTER 21

I slept badly that night, dreaming of dark, shapeless things chasing me and me, unable to run fast enough to get away. I woke feeling tired and a bit frightened.

Florence had refused my offer of a bed, so I'd been alone, with only Nyx for company. After feeling irritated with Rafe for always being in charge, I was unreasonably irritated with him for not being around when I might be in danger. Even Gran had left, along with Silvia and Theodore. There were still vampires downstairs, and they'd assured me they'd come if I called, but I missed having my special friends around.

I shook off my foolishness, showered, had breakfast and dressed defiantly in a bright orange sweater that Alfred had knitted for me. Katie called to say she wouldn't be coming in today. I didn't really blame her.

I got through the day as best I could, serving customers, tidying the shelves, and keeping half an eye on the door, hoping there wasn't a serial killer out there.

Just before five, Sylvia came up. I was delighted to see her. "You're back, already?"

She was gorgeous in a calf-length black coat that looked Italian-designer chic, a hand-knit scarf in black with hints of red, and high-heeled black boots. "Darling, there was nothing holding us in Leeds."

"Did you find out anything?" I was excited to get the latest update.

"We did. But you're grandmother would never forgive me if I told you without her being present."

I glanced at my watch. "I'll close five minutes early and come down."

It didn't take me long to close. Nyx yawned when I shut the blinds and then, after a luxurious stretch, stepped daintily out of her usual spot in the bowl of wools and followed me down to the vampires' underground lair.

Gran let us in, looking very pleased with herself. "How are you holding up, dear?" she asked, searching my face.

"I'm fine. Just a bit nervous."

"We're all on edge. What happens in this street affects all of us." Nyx headed straight for her favorite spot on the couch, and I followed.

Theodore was sitting in one of the red chairs, a computer tablet in his hand. "Good afternoon, Lucy."

"Good afternoon. I'm surprised you're all back so soon."

"Traffic was light. Barely anything at all on the M1. We made good time. Just over three hours going, and a little longer returning." His baby blue eyes twinkled. "Your grandmother was very anxious to get back to you."

"I worry," she said simply. "Now, who wants to tell Lucy what we found out?"

"Why don't you tell her?" Sylvia said, which was generous of her.

"All right." Gran sat beside me and clasped her hands in front of her, the way she did when she was about to tell a story. "We owe so much to Theodore. He was so good at finding things out."

"It was nothing," said Theodore, looking pleased. "Happy to keep my hand in at police work."

"We found the house where Gerald Pettigrew had lived with his wife and two children. Fortunately, the daughter still lives there. She seemed very suspicious and unfriendly when she first answered the door, but once again, Theodore was magnificent." She turned to look at Sylvia, who'd taken off her coat and wore an equally stylish black dress. "And so was Sylvia."

"Oh, nonsense," Sylvia said, "Acting a part still amuses me."

"Sylvia pretended that Gerald Pettigrew had promised to marry her and disappeared, while Theodore said he was a private investigator helping track down the missing man." She chuckled. "That young woman immediately invited us in and poured out her story with no further prompting." Then she sobered and shook her head. "I'm sorry to say that Gerald was not a good father. Or a good man."

"What happened? What did he do?"

"He'd abandoned them, you see. The daughter, Rose was her name, believed he became discontented when she and her brother came along and Gerald's wife no longer wanted to spend her money on extravagant trips and, well, on Gerald. He told them he'd got a job in London that involved travel and was often away. One day, he simply stopped coming home."

"Oh, poor Rose and her brother."

"They were very close to their mother and, I think, they'd seen so little of their father that they didn't miss him, much."

"Did she divorce him?"

Gran sighed. "Theodore, you tell her the rest."

"No. He disappeared and according to Rose, their mother didn't now whether he was alive or dead. She never divorced him or bothered to look for him. She didn't want to marry again so, I suppose, she didn't put in the effort." He looked quite stern. "Though she should have."

"Oh, dear."

He nodded. "I see you've looked ahead, Lucy, and you're quite right. Their mother died. Somehow, Gerald found out and turned up playing the grieving husband."

"The nerve," Sylvia said. She tossed her silver hair. "He must have been a better actor than I."

"Oh, no," Gran said. "No one could be a better actor than you."

Theodore coughed. "To continue, naturally the will had left everything to the two children. Gerald claimed he'd been kept away by his work and the OSA forbid him to say more." He glanced at me. "The Official Secrets Act."

"Oh, I know all about that. Gerald Pettigrew used that line on me, the first day we met."

"Presumably, he hoped his children would share their inheritance with their prodigal father."

"He really was a piece of work," I said.

"When they refused, he challenged the will."

"Ouch. His own children?"

He inclined his head. "When he lost the case, he disappeared again. Rose hasn't seen him in more than six years."

I scratched Nyx under the chin, thinking. "Has Rose been in Oxford recently?"

"No. She's a head teacher at a local school. She hasn't taken a day off in more than a year." He forestalled my next question. "And the brother works on an oil rig in Edmonton, in Canada. He hasn't been back to England in two years."

"So, all we know is that Gerald Pettigrew was a big, fat liar, a terrible father, and a worse husband." I bit my lip. "Did you find any connection between him and Colonel Montague?"

"No."

I GLANCED AT THE DOOR. For a cool shiver was tickling the back of my neck. Sure enough, it opened and in came Rafe. His gaze went straight to mine. "Lucy, are you all right?"

I smiled faintly. "I've been better."

Sylvia walked forward. "I thought you were in Liverpool."

"I cut the trip short. The collection wasn't much. The Dickens wasn't a first edition and badly foxed. I came back as soon as I heard about the murder."

"That was nice of you."

"I've just come from the coroner's office. I have a—" he paused for a moment—"friend on the inside. They put Gerald Pettigrew's time of death between eleven a.m. and two p.m. With the body being inside the fridge but the fridge door open they can't be more exact. They do know, however, that he was killed in the kitchen. The body hadn't been moved."

I said, "I can help narrow down the time of death even further. Because I saw Gerald Pettigrew with my own eyes at noon." I glanced at Rafe who always seemed to know everything the police did. "I saw him with a library book, at least I think it was a library book, did anyone check to see if he returned it?"

"You're right. His library book was returned and time stamped at eleven minutes past noon. The book, if you're interested, was a guide to living aboard a cruise ship full-time."

"Florence said they were planning to get married and travel."

One moment they'd been planning to enjoy their golden years as newlyweds aboard a cruise ship, and now one of them lay in the morgue while the other was being treated by her doctor for shock. Even if he wasn't the man Florence had believed he was, it was still very sad.

Rafe came and stood very close to me and his eyes held mine. "You are very sure, are you, Lucy, that you saw Gerald Pettigrew at noon? It couldn't have been another old gentleman who looked like him?"

I tried to cast my mind back to the moment I'd looked outside and seen the old gentlemen. I said, "Until you asked me, I would have said I was certain it was him. He had the right clothes, right hair and mustache, and I recognized his way of walking."

"But you didn't actually see his face?"

Had I? I closed my eyes. "No. Just the side of his face. He wore a cap on his head, but I'm sure it was him. Besides, I saw the dead body. He was wearing the same clothes."

"Then I'd say that narrows your suspects to Katie and

Mary Watt unless we add in person or persons unknown who may have had a key and wanted Gerald Pettigrew dead."

I didn't want the killer to be either of those lovely women. "I think you must be right. The sleuthing trip to Leeds didn't turn up anything." I was getting tired of amateur sleuthing, tired of being suspicious of everyone. I'd learned that nearly everyone had a dark and deadly secret. Something they'd kill for.

Sylvia yawned. "I'm afraid we've missed our day's sleep. I must have a nap before I go out tonight. So should you, Agnes."

I took the hint. "I'll go, but thank you very much for taking the trip. At least we know more."

Rafe walked out with me and Nyx and we climbed together up into the back room of Cardinal Woolsey's.

"Don't take it too hard, Lucy. We all have to accept the consequences of our own actions."

"I know. I just hate to see those nice old ladies made unhappy."

He smiled slightly. "I've become so used to being surrounded by darkness, being with you is like a glimpse of the sun." To my surprise he put the palm of his hand against my cheek. It was cool, but not unpleasant. He said, "Don't ever let the darkness win."

For a moment he looked at my face so intently I thought he was planning to kiss me. I wasn't sure how I felt about that. He was definitely one of the most attractive men I'd ever known but, if he saw my light, I also saw his darkness.

I suspected he'd done terrible things and was capable of doing many more. The notion sent a shiver of fear down my spine. Perhaps he saw that in my face for he dropped his hand and stepped back. Then he raised his head and said, sounding as sarcastic as a disgruntled lover, "And if I'm not mistaken, here comes your equally sunny detective."

He'd already lifted the trapdoor and was halfway back down into the tunnel when I heard the rap on the front door of the shop.

Rafe might have excellent hearing, but he didn't have x-ray vision. When I went to the front door I discovered not Ian but Mary Watt. I opened the door wondering whether I was greeting a murderer. I wasn't sure I had the stamina for any more drama. "Miss Watt. How are you?"

I knew it was a completely inadequate thing to say but really, what was the correct greeting? How does it feel to be a murderer? Do you know your sister hates you? 'How are you' would have to do. Anyway, she seemed perfectly happy to tell me how she was. She stepped inside my shop and said, "I feel like poor Job, wondering what next will be sent to try me."

"What do you mean? Don't tell me someone else has been killed?"

"Oh nothing as bad as that. But Florence has gone to stay with Elspeth Montague. They were in a book club together for some years. And now they've got their tragedies in common."

I realized the vampire cop was right. If you looked, connections were everywhere.

"Florence won't even look at me. I thought, when she poured out all that anger and bitterness it was just an emotional reaction to the horror of finding Gerald's body. But, you know, I'm beginning to think she really believes I killed him."

I decided, since we were the only two in this lonely building, that asking her if it was true would not be the smartest idea. Instead I said, "She's had a terrible shock. And you wouldn't want her to have to sleep in the building where her lover was killed."

"I suppose not. I don't fancy sleeping there, either. Especially not alone."

And so I found myself offering up my spare room, to the other Miss Watt than the one I planned. To my relief she shook her head. "Oh, that's so sweet of you. And exactly what your grandmother would have done. But I've booked myself into a hotel."

"A hotel? What, here in Oxford?"

"Yes. A very nice hotel. It's full-service. For the first time in years, I shall not be shopping for food, preparing food, or selling food. I'm going to sleep late in the morning. Eat breakfast in bed if I so wish. And, they have a spa."

"Exactly what you need."

"Do you know I've never even been to a spa? I shall have facial. And," she added with the air of one going all the way into the dark side of decadence, "a massage."

I found it hard to imagine this woman who was taking such delight in breakfast in bed and a spa massage could have killed a man. Mary Watt did not strike me as the cold-blooded sort who would kill and then go off to have her pores exfoliated. But what did I know of killers?

She said, "And tomorrow I shall go shopping and buy some new clothes. When you next see me, I should look like a completely different person."

I went upstairs and fed Nyx, who seemed restless and out of sorts. She wouldn't settle on my lap but kept pacing up and down and making that burp noise. I didn't know if I was communicating my restlessness to the cat or it was communicating it to me but I also felt unsettled and slightly jumpy. Something was nagging at me.

I decided to practice one of my spells. There must be something in the grimoire for soothing and restoring peace.

Nyx accompanied me to the kitchen and jumped up onto the counter, which, normally, I tried to discourage. However, I felt that having my familiar present while I tried to brew up a potion could only be a benefit. She didn't seem interested in helping, though, she was still restless and continued making those annoying burp noises. "Do you want to go out?" I asked her, pointing at the open window. She looked at the window and back at me and went burp.

"Well, try and focus, then." I laid my hand on the front of that beautiful heavy book, closed my eyes and recited the words that would open it. A warm musty scent greeted me, something I associated with the Miss Watts. I realized I was smelling mothballs. My eyes flew open. Mothballs? What on earth?

The cat's green eyes widened at the strange smell emanating from the book and she turned and leapt for the top of the fridge. As she did, she managed to knock one of the photographs that Gran always kept stuck on the fridge with a magnet. I leaned to down to the floor and picked up the old snapshot. Gran liked to look at them when she came up here.

The photograph was of me and my mother. I was probably about six or seven and we were standing, both wearing shorts. My dad had obviously sent the snap to Gran because he'd written on the back, "Look at those legs! Like mother like daughter."

I felt like an electric shock had run up my arm and I

gasped aloud. Rapidly, I put the picture back onto the fridge and closed the grimoire knowing the spell would reset immediately to keep it safe from prying eyes or hands.

I'd been such a fool. Now I knew what had been nagging at me. I ran down into the shop and grabbed a midrange wool blend that we often recommended for beginners. It was a nice blue color. Grabbed some needles, also good for beginners, and, making sure no one was looking in the windows, I uttered an incantation that I had just taken from the book.

The needles got busy knitting. It was a pleasure to watch them doing their work so effortlessly, without me getting in the way. I glanced at my watch, I didn't have a great deal of time. I pointed to the knitting needles and commanded, "*Velox*". And saw the speed increase so quickly the knitting needles were blurring before my eyes. I waited until there was about six inches of stocking stitch. I stopped the knitting needles and said, "Nodo chaos." It was as though unseen fingers went into those perfectly knitted stitches and twisted and tangled every one of them. At the end of the destruction, the piece looked exactly as though I had knitted it myself.

I phoned Katie and was thankful that she picked up my call right away. "Katie, I've got a problem. I've been practicing another piece of knitting and I've made the most awful mess of it. I really need the distraction, I've got to find a way to calm my nerves, and this tangle is only making me feel worse. Could I come over and get you to straighten it out for me?"

CHAPTER 22

*T*here was a slight pause. I'm sure she was trying to think of a way to turn me down, but I sounded so clearly distraught that she said, "All right. Yes, of course, come on over."

I threw the mess into a bag, got onto my bicycle and rode to where they were living, in a basement flat in Summertown.

I realized I was being impulsive and probably foolish, still, before I went in, I sent a text to Ian telling him of my suspicions. No doubt he'd tell me to mind my own business.

I knocked on the door and Katie let me in right away. The flat was pretty grim even for student digs. The basement door opened directly into the main living room, which contained a shabby two-seater couch in front of a table with a small television. In the corner was an eating table that doubled as a desk. A fairly new looking laptop sat on top of it as well as salt-and-pepper shakers. Opening off this room was a tiny kitchen and another door that was presumably the bathroom. A further door was partly ajar and I could see a double bed, and a chest of drawers and what looked like an old wardrobe. Katie was alone. She held up her own piece of knitting and smiled. "I was doing the same thing. I find it very soothing, too."

"It's nice of you to let me come. I really wanted the distraction of knitting, but I made another mess of it."

"Jim will be home soon. I've just got his dinner warming in the oven. Do you want a beer? Or tea?"

I needed to get rid of her for a few minutes to do some sleuthing. "Tea would be wonderful."

"Of course," she said. And went into the kitchen, saying over her shoulder, "Make yourself at home."

"Thanks. I'll just use the loo."

Instead of going into the bathroom, however, I ducked into the bedroom. My heart pounded and I felt dreadful taking advantage of her hospitality in this way, but I had to know the truth. I had to know if my hunch was right.

I pulled open the wardrobe doors and saw a few pairs of jeans hanging on hangers, a couple of cotton dresses, a raincoat, an umbrella shoved in the back and what looked like extra bedding. Making sure she was still in the kitchen I dashed to the chest of drawers. They were cheap pressboard but new enough that the drawers opened soundlessly. The first contained nothing but socks and underwear. The second was packed with his and hers T-shirts, and two jumpers, one of which I remembered Jim wearing. I was about to try the third drawer when I heard Katie's puzzled voice call, "Lucy?"

Damn.

I came out of the bedroom looking as nonchalant as I could. "Sorry. I was looking for the bathroom."

Silently she pointed at the bathroom door and with a

nervous giggle I went in. Please let her just think I was a harmless snoop, I thought, making a production of washing my hands. Over the sound of the running water I eased open the medicine cabinet and took a good look inside, I even checked out the tiny wastepaper basket.

When I came out Katie said, "I wasn't sure if you liked milk and sugar, but I'm afraid we haven't got any milk."

"Clear's fine. Really, I'm more worried about the knitting."

"All right, then," she said. "Let's have a look."

Katie pulled the tangled mess of knitting out of the bag and smoothed it carefully on her denim-clad knee. "You weren't kidding. You did make a mess of this."

"I think it was the stress. I don't know what I was doing."

She eased out the knitting needle and, as she'd done before, began to pull out all the stitches. She said, "The first thing you need to do is learn to lessen your tension. You pull the wool far too tight. Maybe you should just practice making a square, over and over until you get the hang of the right tension. And learn to keep track of your stitches."

She sounded so patient I thought how much I'd like it if she'd offer knitting classes at my shop. Apart from my vampire knitting club I didn't have any regular classes because I didn't know how to knit. I needed someone like Katie, someone who could both knit and teach.

She began casting on a set of stitches. When I glanced at the clock I saw that it was nearly seven. I said, "Look, why don't I take that home, and work on it myself? You're quite right, I'd be much better to just do a couple of small squares. Perhaps you can take a look at them in the morning?"

"Don't you want me to get you started now?" She seemed

quite surprised, as well she might, as I had specifically come over to visit her so that she could do that for me. I told her the truth, "Jim will be home soon. And he won't want to find me here."

But it was already too late. Katie's less acute ears soon picked up what mine had already registered. She said, "I think that's him, now."

Sure enough, through the window, I saw a pair of legs descending. She got up and went to the door, opening it so that she could say, almost as he walked in, "Hi, Jim. Lucy's here. She needed some help with her knitting."

Giving me a cheery wave, he said, "How ya goin'?"

But I couldn't answer him. I was staring at those trousers, and the shoes. I had discovered that shock made people do very stupid things, and it made me off the scale stupid. "You didn't bother to get rid of the shoes."

His smile went rigid, but he decided to deliberately misunderstand me. "You've got a sharp eye. You're right. These are my character's shoes, for the part I'm playing." He still had a trace of make-up on his face, where he hadn't cleaned it off properly.

"But that's not the only part you played, is it?" I asked him.

"What are you getting at?"

"You know, you nearly got away with it. But that wasn't Gerald Pettigrew I saw walking past so conveniently right when the noon bells were ringing, was it? It was you."

He looked at Katie and said, "What's she on about? Have you two been round the pub?"

Katie shook her head. "I don't know. She got her knitting in a tangle. She was one of the people who found poor Miss

Watt's boyfriend murdered yesterday. I think it's turned her head a bit."

He looked at me with cold eyes. "Terrible end for the old bloke."

I looked at his face, closely. "He wasn't just an old bloke, was he? Gerald Pettigrew, or whatever he called himself in Australia, was your father."

There was terrible silence. Katie said, sounding unsure, "Lucy, maybe you should go home."

But Jim positioned himself in front of the door and crossed his arms over his chest. Thick arms. Thick chest. "No. I think Lucy'd better explain what she's talking about."

In my own defense, I don't think I would have tackled him like this if Katie hadn't been there. I didn't really think he would try and hurt me in front of her, and I was fairly sure he wouldn't try and do away with us both. It wasn't not much of a defense, but it was all I had. The thing was, I saw exactly what had happened now and so clearly, but he was the only person who could confirm what I'd guessed.

"I thought when I first met you that you seemed vaguely familiar. Do you have his walk naturally? Or did you copy it like any good actor?"

He shrugged and said, "Bit of both, I imagine."

"You have his teeth, too."

He lifted his shoulders as though he couldn't care less.

"Gerald Pettigrew abandoned you when you were a child. It destroyed your family, didn't it?"

"Jim? What's this? What's going on?" Katie broke in.

But Jim was looking at me. "It killed Mum. She was a good woman, and after he left, she never got over the shock. So, yeah, I tracked the old bastard down. Found out my mum wasn't the only one he'd used and abandoned. He was an evil man, a predator. He went after women with a little money and charmed it out of them. Then left them with nothing."

Katie put her hand to her mouth. "Oh, Jim. Why didn't you tell me?"

He looked at her then and his mouth quirked in a half smile. "You wouldn't have come with me if I had."

"You followed Gerald Pettigrew to Oxford."

"Yeah. I'd been watching him. When I saw him romancing old Miss Watt, everything fell into place like it'd been stage-managed. The lady was really taken with my old man, and that meant she couldn't manage the kitchen anymore. I'd been trying to figure out how to get inside, but not so he'd see much of me." He laughed, mockingly. "Not that he'd recognize his own son."

"Oh, Jim," Katie said again. I thought she was beginning to put two and two together.

"I'd heard they only hired waitresses at Elderflower, one of the old girls did all the cooking, when I overheard a row and realized she'd not been doing her job properly, because of Gerald. I saw it as an opportunity. We were the answer to her sister's prayers."

"When did your father suspect you?"

"I don't think he ever did. He was so full of himself, that when the wrong bloke got poisoned he never twigged that it was meant for him. It was only later, after the police questioned them, that I think he suspected the other Miss Watt. She knew what he was, you see."

"She told you this?"

"Didn't have to. They had a row in the kitchen when I was

outside having a smoke. Didn't know I was out there, listening."

Katie staggered over to the couch and sank into it. Her face was drained of color. "You poisoned Colonel Montague?"

"That was your fault, kiddo." He turned to me. "I told her take the tray to table six, and, just to make sure she got the right table, I said it was the old bloke in the window."

"But there were two old blokes sitting side-by-side in window tables. And Katie mixed up the order."

Katie made an awful, choking sound. "I think I might be sick."

Neither of us so much as glanced her way. I said, "So, the second time you tried to kill your father, you did it yourself so there could be no mistakes."

"Yeah. And, I wanted him to know who did it. I wanted to look him in the eye and tell him what he'd done. And I wanted to watch him die. I don't care what happens to me now, it was worth it."

He let out a breath. "I'm sorry about the colonel, though. Sorry about you."

Katie jumped up and said, "No! Jim, no."

He looked at her and his eyes softened. "Katie, love, I have to kill her. And then you and me'll go on the run. I'm sorry, love, but there it is."

He seemed to think for a moment and I saw him, unconsciously I think, flex his fingers. He said to me, "Now, you come in the bedroom with me, and don't make a fuss. I'll make it nice and easy."

I shook my head, trying to think of a spell that would stop him in his tracks, but my mind was chaos. "No. I don't think I will." I'd heard some sounds outside that suggested I was not alone. I screamed. I didn't get much of the scream out, because Jim launched himself at me, pushing us both to the grubby couch, trying to get his hands around my throat. Katie yelled and began hitting him with her fists. I don't think she did much damage, but I appreciated the support.

Fortunately, before he was able to get his hands fully round my neck there was a commotion outside and the door burst open. He was pulled bodily off me and in the next instant, he was face down on the floor, with two uniformed police officers holding him down. One handcuffed him while the other read him his rights. I drew in a shaky breath.

Ian helped me sit up. He looked grim, almost angry. "Lucy? Can you breathe?"

I nodded.

He said, curtly, to someone behind him, "Call an ambulance." Then to me, "We'll get you to hospital. Make sure you're all right."

I put a hand on his arm. Found it rigid with tension. "No. Really. He barely touched me. It was Jim I saw at noon, you see. I should've realized the minute Katie said to me, that he looked like a completely different person when he was dressed up to go to the play. Of course, that was his alibi. He dressed up as his own father, with a wig and mustache, clothes from the prop room. But by then Gerald Pettigrew was already dead."

"You're right."

I clutched his arm, I needed to be sure he understood me. "It was Jim who killed Gerald Pettigrew. Gerald was his father."

He said very gently, "Yes, Lucy. We know." He shook his

head at me. "We were collecting evidence. We'd have got him without you nearly getting yourself killed."

It turned out the Gerald Pettigrew had bilked at least four women out of their money, often their self-respect and, in the case of Jim's mother, her life. I tried not to wish anyone harm, but Gerald Pettigrew had been a bad man. At least now Florence Watt would not become his next victim.

Katie stood in the corner, clutching my knitting to her the way a child would a beloved stuffed animal. Her eyes were wide and she seemed to be in shock. I looked at Ian. "And Katie?"

He shook his head. "As far as we can tell, she knew nothing about Jim's plans. I think he used her as a smokescreen."

They took Jim away, of course. Ian said, "I've got to go."

I nodded, understanding they probably wanted to question Jim immediately, try for a full confession. I turned down his repeated offer of the ambulance, or of someone to see me home. The streets of Oxford were much safer, now. I'd be safe to ride home.

I offered to stay with Katie, or take her back to my place, but she insisted she preferred to be left alone. There were no words of comfort I could offer her. So I just said, "I'm so sorry."

She offered me the knitting back but I shook my head. "Why don't you keep it? At least it will keep your hands busy."

"What will happen to Jim?"

"I really don't know. If he doesn't confess, he'll go to trial, of course, but other than that, I have no idea."

"I'll go to the Australian Consulate and see if he can be

extradited to Australia. I think he'd be happier at home. Even if he is in jail."

Any kind of plan gave her something useful to do. I told her I thought that was an excellent idea and then, as I was leaving, she said, "I didn't know. I didn't even guess. He's a good bloke, you know. Funny, and kind."

I didn't bother to tack on the obvious addendum, funny and kind and had murdered two people, one presumably by accident. I simply said good night and left.

It was full on night by now. As I rode my bike home, I felt a slight chill in my neck that told me I wasn't alone. I didn't bother turning around. I was fairly certain I wouldn't be able to see him, but I knew that Rafe, in his own quaintly chivalrous way, was seeing me home.

By the time I'd put my bike away, he was waiting at the front door of the shop. I let him in and said, "I'm going upstairs and I'm going to open a bottle of wine. Do you drink wine?"

"Yes. I'll keep you company."

Gran and Sylvia were no doubt still sleeping, so I was happy to have the company. I dug out a cold bottle of California Chardonnay that I'd bought because I was homesick. He looked at the label and shook his head. "California wine, Lucy? Really? When across the channel you have some of the greatest vineyards in the world."

I rolled my eyes and got out two glasses. "No doubt you're a wine connoisseur, as well."

"Of course. I'll treat you to something out of my cellar one of these days."

I hoped we were still talking about wine. I didn't want to dwell on what vampires kept in their cellars.

CHAPTER 23

The sound of twenty pairs of knitting needles clicking away was soothing, I found, as we all settled for the meeting of the vampire knitting club. Silence Buggins was visiting friends in New York, which was why we had any silence at all. Perhaps we all relished those few moments as we found our rhythm, checked where we were in the pattern, or just enjoyed creating something new.

Gran broke the silence. "How is poor Florence Watt, Lucy? I wish I could see her. It must've been such a terrible shock to find out that the man she almost married was such a dreadful user of women."

"I think it will take her a while to get over the shock, but it helped so much that I was able to share with her some of the information you found on your trip to Leeds. I think, knowing she wasn't the only one who was duped by Gerald Pettigrew helped her not feel such an old fool."

Gran finished a complicated looking row. "Awkward for

her, having accused her elder sister of murder. Are they speaking again?"

"I think so. They did talk about putting the shop up for sale and moving on but I think neither of them can imagine what they'd do with themselves with all that free time. Besides, staying busy and connected with the world is the best way to put this tragedy behind them."

"Very sensible."

"One thing I did hear, though, is that they are agreed that when they re-open they'll go back to the classic menu. No more white chocolate or ginger scones or prawn salads for the Elderberry Tea Shop."

Gran's eyes twinkled. "No, indeed. They found out what letting a chef with newfangled ideas into their kitchen could lead to."

Alfred said, "I am sorry that poor Colonel Montague was accidentally killed, though."

Sylvia smiled. "Well, you may be, but I don't think the widow's too sad. She's had the decorators in and she's having the house remodeled. She bought herself a new car and she and her children are planning a holiday in the south of France. So somebody's finally spending the old miser's money."

I was able to tell them that I'd heard from the Irish woman and Mrs. Montague had done the right thing. She'd agreed to hire a private nurse for Eileen and had settled some of the colonel's money on the woman he'd wronged and his grown daughter.

"And what about Miss Everly?"

"She's got a new fellow. Her three friends from St. Hilda's put up a profile online and she's met someone."

"So all's well that ends well."

I groaned. "Except that I'm looking for another new assistant."

"Oh no. And Katie was so good. Can't you keep her on?"

"I begged her to stay, but she's sticking by Jim. She's helping with his defense, and she's hoping to get him extradited to Australia. She said she hasn't got time to work in the shop. I think she doesn't want to be too close to the scene of the crime, either."

"Katie turned out to be brave and loyal. Qualities that would have kept Gerald Pettigrew alive if only he'd had them."

"They're holding Jim in prison here for now."

Gran said, "That poor young man will be very cold in prison if he's used to Australia. I bet he'd like a nice jumper."

Twenty vampire heads rose in the excitement of fresh humans to knit for. Alfred said, "Oh, and the poor young lady, she'll need jumpers, too."

"Lucy, dear, do you know what colors Katie likes?"

Thank you for reading. I hope you enjoyed Lucy's latest adventure. Keep reading for a sneak peek of the next mystery.

A Note from Nancy

Dear Reader,

Thank you for reading the Vampire Knitting Club series. I am so grateful for all the enthusiasm this series has received. I have plenty more stories about Lucy and her undead knitters planned for the future.

I hope you'll consider leaving a review and please tell your friends who like cozy mysteries.

Review on Amazon, Goodreads or BookBub.

Your support is the wool that helps me knit up these yarns. Turn the page for a sneak peek of Crochet and Cauldrons, Book 3 of the Vampire Knitting Club.

Until next time,
Happy Reading,

Nancy

CROCHET AND CAULDRONS

© 2018 NANCY WARREN

Chapter 1

"Good afternoon, Mrs. Winters," I said, walking into the corner grocer at the top of Harrington Street, in Oxford. It was convenient, only up the block from where Cardinal Woolsey's Knitting Shop was located.

Our little corner of Oxford was my favorite part of that ancient city. There was one college on the street, but it wasn't famous. There were no world-class restaurants or fancy hotels. No celebrity had been born or died here. It wasn't even in the oldest part of the city. What Harrington Street had, was rows of tiny shops and houses that had stood there for about two hundred and fifty years. And one of them was mine.

I'd only been running Cardinal Woolsey's for a few months and I was still discovering new quirks and oddities in the neighborhood—and that was just the people! Of course, since I was both young and American, I often had to explain

229

how I came to own a quaint, old knitting shop. The easiest explanation, and the truth, was that I'd inherited the shop when my beloved grandmother died.

The slightly more complicated explanation, also true, was that before she was all- the-way-dead, one of Gran's vampire friends turned her. So, I ran the shop with a great deal of interference from a group of bored know-it-all vampires who were crazy good knitters.

"How's business, Lucy?" asked Mrs. Winters. She was inclined to be nosy.

"Fine. I'm thinking of branching into selling designer knitted garments, possibly on the Internet." The vampire knitting club turned out the most incredible work at warp speed and I hoped that if I could keep them busy enough, they might have less time and energy to interfere in my life. It was a faint hope, but I was clinging to it.

"That's a lovely sweater you're wearing," she said, peering at me closer. "Did you knit it yourself?"

I swallowed the urge to snort. My attempts to knit were about as good as my track record at keeping an assistant. Pitiful. The sweater I wore was gorgeous. A deep purple background with an indescribable, but beautiful, geometric pattern of diamonds and squares in complimentary shades. The sweater had been made by Doctor Christopher Weaver, a local GP and vampire. The vampires took turns knitting me sweaters, shawls, and dresses to wear in the store. Every day I turned up in something amazing, which I usually only wore once, as there was always another new creation waiting for me to slip into. That's why I was thinking of branching out into ready-made items.

"I need a new assistant, though," I said, holding up the

advertisement I'd made. "Do you mind if I pin the job posting on your community board?"

I'd also put the ad online and I'd posted a help wanted sign in my front window, but everybody in the neighborhood checked the community board at Full Stop, the grocer's. It was the best place to find a violin teacher, a roommate, or a job.

However, pinning a notice up always had a price. Especially as I kept putting up the same one: "Shop Assistant wanted at Cardinal Woolsey's Knitting Shop. Must be an experienced knitter with retail experience." I went through assistants the way an allergy sufferer with a bad cold went through tissues.

I waited. Sure enough, she raised her brows in fake shock. "Good heavens. Another assistant?" She leaned across the counter, past the display of lottery tickets and a plastic basket of mini packs of Chocolate Buttons and Jelly Babies, all ready for Halloween. But her voice was so piercing I'm sure they could hear her at the top of the Radcliffe Camera. "It's very important to keep consistency. Rapid staff turnover isn't good for your business's reputation." She smiled at me in a very patronizing way. "I'm sure you don't mind me giving you a hint, my dear. Only, I've been in business a great deal longer than you have."

I could have told her that my first assistant had been a psychopath, my second assistant had freaked out after seeing my supposedly dead grandmother wandering around the shop, and my third had gone back to Australia to be with her boyfriend, the murderer, but I held my tongue and tried to look grateful for the unwanted advice.

Then, as though belatedly remembering how I had come

to lose my third assistant, she said, "Of course, it's all been so dreadful with that fuss at the tea shop."

It takes a very special person to call two murders a fuss.

I smiled sweetly. "Can I put up my notice?" It was a Sunday afternoon and I was spending my only day of the week off doing catching-up chores, like vacuuming, and advertising for a new assistant.

"Yes, of course, dear. And I'll keep my eye out, too, for the right person. What sort of employee do you have in mind?"

I knew exactly the sort of person I wanted. I could picture her in my mind. "I'm looking for a middle-aged woman, perhaps someone whose children have grown and is looking for part-time work. She has to be an excellent knitter, of course, have some experience in sales, and if she's got teaching experience that would be even better. She must be available to work Saturdays." I pictured a plump woman who wore cardigans that she'd knitted herself.

She'd be motherly, the kind of person who could dispense life advice as easily as she could turn a sleeve or knit a picture of Santa and the reindeer into a child's red sweater. *Jumper*, I corrected myself mentally.

I felt certain she was out there, my fantasy knitting shop assistant. Until she showed up, I was making do on my own with sporadic assistance from some of the vampire ladies who had never been known locally when they were alive. Naturally, my grandmother was desperate to be involved, but I only let her help with the stock-taking and tidying up once the store was closed and I'd pulled the blinds.

Having tacked up my notice and purchased fresh bread and milk for me, and half a dozen cans of tuna for Nyx, my black cat familiar, who is very particular about her diet, I walked the short distance back to my shop, my reusable cloth shopping bag swinging from my hand. Now that my chores were done, I was looking forward to an afternoon studying magic spells, with the help of my family grimoire. My witch cousin and great aunt kept encouraging me to join their coven, but I was hesitant to do so, with so few witchy skills to offer.

The truth was, I seemed to get thrown into things I wasn't very good at. For instance, I owned a knitting shop, and I couldn't knit. I'd tried and tried. Gran said I didn't focus properly, but I found it very difficult to keep my attention on a couple of metal sticks and constantly looping wool around them while keeping count. I couldn't figure out how anyone kept their focus. My creations, whether attempts at scarves, socks, or sweaters, all ended up looking like variations of the sea urchin or hedgehog family. Sometimes I thought I should invent a line of knitted hedgehogs. I could really go to town.

Gran said I came from a long line of illustrious witches. I didn't know what my descendants might say of me, in the future, but I didn't think they'd use the word illustrious. My potions didn't turn out, I'd forget my spells halfway through, and I tended to blow things up. Not on purpose.

Order your copy today! *Crochet and Cauldrons* is Book 3 in the Vampire Knitting Club series.

ALSO BY NANCY WARREN

The best way to keep up with new releases, plus enjoy bonus content and prizes is to join Nancy's newsletter at nancywarren.net

The Vampire Knitting Club

Stitches and Witches, Vampire Knitting Club Book 2

Crochet and Cauldrons, Vampire Knitting Club Book 3

Stockings and Spells, Vampire Knitting Club Book 4

Purls and Potions Vampire Knitting Club Book 5

Toni Diamond Mysteries

Toni is a successful saleswoman for Lady Bianca Cosmetics in this series of humorous cozy mysteries. Along with having an eye for beauty and a head for business, Toni's got a nose for trouble and she's never shy about following her instincts, even when they lead to murder.

Frosted Shadow Toni Diamond Mysteries, Book One

Ultimate Concealer Toni Diamond Mysteries, Book Two

Midnight Shimmer Toni Diamond Mysteries, Book Three

A Diamond Choker For Christmas A Toni Diamond Mysteries Novella

The Almost Wives Club

An enchanted wedding dress is a matchmaker in this series of romantic comedies where five runaway brides find out who the best men really are!

The Almost Wives Club: Kate

Second Hand Bride

Bridesmaid for Hire

The Wedding Flight

If the Dress Fits

Take a Chance series

Meet the Chance family, a cobbled together family of eleven kids who are all grown up and finding their ways in life and love.

Kiss a Girl in the Rain Take a Chance, Book 1

Iris in Bloom Take a Chance, Book 2

Blueprint for a Kiss Take a Chance, Book 3

Every Rose Take a Chance, Book 4

Love to Go Take a Chance, Book 5

Chance Encounter Prequel

ABOUT THE AUTHOR

Nancy Warren is the USA Today Bestselling author of more than 70 novels. She's originally from Vancouver, Canada, though she tends to wander and has lived in England, Italy and California at various times. While living in Oxford she dreamed up The Vampire Knitting Club. She's currently in Bath, UK, where she often pretends she's Jane Austen. Or at least a character in a Jane Austen novel. Favorite moments include being the answer to a crossword puzzle clue in Canada's National Post newspaper, being featured on the front page of the New York Times when her book Speed Dating launched Harlequin's NASCAR series, and being nominated three times for Romance Writers of America's RITA award. She has an MA in Creative Writing from Bath Spa University. She's an avid hiker, loves chocolate and most of all, loves to hear from readers! The best way to stay in touch is to sign up for Nancy's newsletter at www.nancywarren.net.

To learn more about Nancy and her books
www.nancywarren.net

2 1982 03150 4537

CPSIA information can be obtained
at www.ICGtesting.com
Printed in the USA
LVHW051432080320
649329LV00009B/517

9 781928 145493